THE UNCLAIMED LUGGAGE

AND OTHER STORIES

THE UNCLAIMED LUGGAGE

AND OTHER STORIES

SAYANTAN GUPTA

LiFi Publications Pvt. Ltd.
New Delhi

Published by:
LiFi Publications Pvt. Ltd.
211, 2nd Floor, Gagandeep
12, Rajendra Place, New Delhi - 110 008, India
Phone : (011) 2574 1000
E-mail : info@lifipublications.com
Web : www.lifipublications.com

ISBN 13: 978-93-82536-06-2 ISBN 10: 93-82536-06-X

First published in 2013

Cataloging in Publication Data—DK
[Courtesy: D.K. Agencies (P) Ltd. <docinfo@dkagencies.com>]

Gupta, Sayantan, 1955-
The unclaimed luggage and other stories / Sayantan Gupta.
p. cm.
Short stories.
ISBN 9789382536062
ISBN 938253606X

1. Short stories, Indic (English). I. Title.

DDC 823.92 23

Printed in India by D.K. Fine Art Press (P) Ltd., Delhi - 52

I dedicate this book to the memory of my father,
Late Samarendra Nath Gupta, at whose feet
I learnt the basics of the English language.
I wish he was here today, beside me.
I miss him always.

Contents

Preface

This is a motley collection of short stories. The stories included here are all of different moods, some of them funny, some outright hilarious, some sad, and some, I do not know what.

Writing a short story, though very rewarding in itself, is one of the toughest things on earth. I have written a novel or two, or a poem here and a ballad there, and I can vouch for it. There is no scope of rambling on and on or the reader will throw the book away, unread. There is no space to build up a character or a situation, but all has to be there. That is why I find it to be a tall order.

No fiction on earth is totally fictitious. Maybe more knowledgeable person will disagree, but I feel that matter cannot be created from a vacuum. There are incidents happening all around, snippets of overheard conversation, news items read in the newspaper or heard over the TV, anything can spark off a story to explode in the author's head. In this context I would like to proclaim that my stories too, had not been created from zero. But everything about them, incidents, characters, all are results of my fevered imagination.

English is a language I love, next to my mother tongue. It is no longer a 'foreign' language, but is spoken by millions of Indians as a mother tongue and is read by more. Indian writing in English has come to stay, and it has enriched the field of Indian literature in more ways than one. Therefore, I write in this language as much as I do in my mother tongue, Bengali.

While writing these stories and compiling them, I am indebted to my wife, Puspita, and our daughters, Parnasha and Shamayita, for having put up with my idiosyncrasies. All of them take immense interest in my works and are abreast with all the developments taking place.

Short stories were not my forte. I am ever grateful to my friend, Prof. Dr. Bina Biswas, Head of the Department of English, Jawaharlal Nehru Technological University, Hyderabad, for first showing me the ropes.

I am also grateful to Sri Rakesh Sharma ji of LiFi Publications for giving me a break. He had been my pillar of strength, always providing encouragement and support. I acknowledge the roles of the Management, the Editorial Board and other staff of LiFi Publications in making this book see the light of the day.

All said and done, a book is only as good as the readers find it to be. if I score on that count, I shall be very happy indeed.

Sayantan Gupta
Malda

1

The Unclaimed Luggage

There was a great commotion in a corner of the platform. A big crowd had gathered. Amongst the teeming crowds khaki caps could be seen bobbing up about like buoys in the sea. The Railway Police had their hands full. Their number was pitiably low, compared to the number of inquisitive onlookers who had gathered around. The crowd, however, was not unruly at all. They calmly gathered around looking at an object placed on the floor. The crowd had taken the shape of a ring. No geometric shape other than this was conceivable, as the police had taken great care to cordon off the immediate vicinity of the bag. This was a not-too-large station where most express and mail trains stopped, but some did not. The number of policemen was not large. They did not have the posts and yellow tape to cordon off an area efficiently. So the officers used constables instead. These constables, positioned at strategic points around the object in question, had cordoned off the area quite effectively. The station master had sent a telegram to the nearest big junction and a special train would be coming soon carrying a proper, well equipped bomb squad and a sniffer dog. The crowd was agog with excitement.

The object in question was a simple gunny bag with the open end covered by a *gamchha* or hand loom towel and tied up with a piece of string. From the outside it appeared to contain some boxes. The question was not what the bag contained. The question was whom it could belong to. There was apparently no claimant. Ranjan had seen it there, in a relatively quiet corner of the platform and it had excited his imagination. He had kept a cool eye on it for quite a long time. It had already cost him three unnecessary cups of tea, when he decided that enough was enough. Like any other good citizen of this country, who travels regularly by train, he was perfectly aware as to what needed to be done if one came across an unclaimed piece of luggage in the railway premises. This subject had been hammered into the consciousness of commuters, through the aegis of huge hoardings strategically placed all over. Once he was sure that it was unclaimed, Ranjan had informed the nearest man in black, aka a railway official and soon all chips began falling in place. The railway man informed the station master, who, in turn, telephoned the Railway Police outpost. The Railway Police took immediate charge and afterwards realized that they did not have a bomb squad or sniffer dog. The officer-in-charge telephoned his counterpart in the town police. But they too, were not equipped to tackle such an emergency. So, the Railway Police requested the station master to send a telegram to senior officials on their behalf, as their wireless was not functioning and the officer-in-charge did not have much balance left in his mobile.

Like vultures sniffing out carrion, the media sniffed out a story at the station platform. They swarmed around in a large number, looking mightily important in their press badges, cameras, movie cameras, notebooks and pencils. Failing to elicit any response from the constables and railwaymen alike, they pounced on the station master, who hid himself behind a barricade of "no comments", and the officer-in-charge of the Railway Police, who had little but a scowl to offer. A report in the media, on the treatment of a suspected wagon-breaker had dragged the policeman to the precincts of the Human Rights Commission only three weeks ago and that rankled. Not to be outdone, the undaunted scribes pounced upon the gathered onlookers and started taking byte after byte. The cameramen, however, had a field day and shot still and video pictures of the bag and the crowd from all conceivable angles.

Sudhir was disconsolate. He had come to this town over the weekend and was on his way home by the afternoon express train. His ancestral home was in this town. Now his mother stayed here with his younger brother and his family of three. He, for himself, stayed in a neighbouring town, where he worked in the State Electricity Board office and his wife worked as a primary School teacher. Sudhir had spent a good weekend in his house and had a wonderful time with his mother and brother's family. He had also met a few of his old school friends, and it had felt really great. When he was leaving, his mother had packed a container with his favourite mutton preparation, and two other smaller tins with coconut sweets that she had made for her grandchildren. She had put all these goodies in a gunny bag, covered the open end with a towel and tied the ends with a string so that it could be carried easily. Sudhir had no other piece of luggage with him except for a small overnighter and this additional bag was of no problem.

At the station Sudhir came to know that the train he was supposed to go by, was a couple of hours late. He went up to the enquiry office to get the latest update. A big crowd had assembled in front of the enquiry office. Sudhir jostled and elbowed there but could not reach the window. He then set the bag down and pushed forward to get news of his train. Indeed it was late. He pushed out of the crowd and bent down to pick up his bag, but it was not there. Sudhir was frantic. He searched here and there. But the bag was nowhere to be found.

Kelo and Haripada were two bosom friends right from childhood till now. Both were in the same vocation and both did their work well. Both were well respected in their fraternity. Both were highly skilled thieves whose field of activity was the railway platform. Today Kelo was crestfallen because he had not made a single 'kill' since morning. All the passengers had become extremely vigilant, much to his chagrin. But just now he had heard an announcement that the express train was late. Kelo brightened up. From his vast experience he knew that the passengers of trains that are late became more fed up, annoyed and less alert. He thanked his stars and the gods above, for providing this golden opportunity. He began prowling through the crowded platform from one end to the other. But all his efforts were in vain. Now he really missed his sidekick, Haripada. Dejected, he went over to the tea stall for his daily free half cup of tea. It was part of the deal he had with Ramsharan, the stall owner. There would be no pilferage of any article in Ramsharan's shop and Ramsharan had to supply free tea to Kelo and Haripada. As an insurance policy it was good enough. So far Ramsharan had kept his word, as Kelo and Haripada theirs.

"Ram bhai," called Kelo as he drew up a stool close to the stall owner. "Give me my tea."

"*Kya re* Kelo? Is business down today?"

"It happens, bhai. It happens. But don't worry. In our line morning does not always show the day." Kelo was philosophical. Ramsharan handed him his scheduled half cup of tea. It was freshly prepared and scalding hot. Kelo was just blowing into it to cool it, when something came to his notice. From where he sat, the enquiry office could be seen clearly. A large number of people had gathered in front of that office, but that was not important. That was expected whenever a train was late. But the thing that drew his attention was a gunny bag which had been left unattended, close to the office. Kelo put down his cup with the tea untouched and bade adieu to Ramsharan.

When Kelo moved out on a mission he resembled an unseen wisp of smoke. He had the uncanny ability of mingling with the milling crowds and becoming nearly invisible. Unseen by all he slunk up to the enquiry, picked the bag up and moved away nonchalantly, tonelessly whistling a tuneless number.

Haripada accosted him near the end of the platform.

"Hey," said he. "I'd been searching for you the whole day. Where have you been?"

"Hunting," replied Kelo, gesturing towards the bag he held in his hand.

"Huh! Only this puny bag and you call it hunting! Come along. I've landed a big fish before the morning mail train and that calls for celebration. I've brought a bottle. Pocha and Babla are waiting for us. Come to Number 5." Number five was platform number five. It was usually deserted for the better part of the day.

Kelo put the bag down in a deserted area and looked about him. Apparently no one had seen him. It was the rule amongst the thieves working at the station area not to keep stolen articles with them for long. That is why Kelo put it down and mentally marked the spot where he had kept it. The bag did not appear to contain anything of great value and it would keep till he returned from his drinking spree. He was not worried about his professional colleagues. The thieves in this part were honest and did not touch the articles of the other thieves. The attractions offered at number 5 were too much to ignore. Following his friend, Kelo jumped down on to the railway track and ran to his tryst with the bottle with fried gram, onions and green chilli. The bag could wait, but the beverage would not. It was then that Ranjan had noticed the bag for the first time.

The officer-in-charge, Khan, was deeply distressed. The train with the bomb-squad and sniffer dogs was held up at the junction due to unfathomable reasons. So, keeping the crowd in control would have to continue for God only knows how long! Added to it was the news that the local minister, Mr. Narayan Tribedi would be coming to the station soon, within the next hour or so, to catch the evening express. Propriety demanded that he should get this platform cleared before he came in. But how, he had no idea. Khan opened the topmost drawer of his table and fished out a strip of antacid tablet. He popped a couple of them in his mouth and started chewing. Something had to be done. But he knew not, what. He put on his cap, tightened his belt, called out to the second officer to remain in charge and walked out. He was determined to set everything right by the time the minister arrived.

Mr. Narayan Tribedi was the veritable uncrowned king in these parts. The opposition spread a lot of rumours and stories about him, but he was in no way perturbed by them. He was a billionaire, who had risen from the rank and file of his party by sheer hard work, diligence and a strong pair of arms. Detractors said that most of his riches were ill-gotten, but that did not bother him. He had a very efficient book keeper who maintained his books so well that even the Election Commission could not find any irregularity there. To his followers, he was a great philanthropist, and to his opponents he was a philanderer par excellence. His rise in state politics had been astronomical and mainly due to the fact that he never lost an opportunity at keeping up public relations. He was a darling of the media too, for with him around there was never a dull moment. Today he was going to Kolkata to attend the Assembly Session. He was going by the evening train.

Kelo was feeling confident and jubilant. After a couple of quick gulps and another two pegs, he felt at the top of the world. He stood up and stretched. Amidst noisy protestations from his cronies he vaulted down the platform on to the tracks in a bid to recover his bag from number one. As he was about to jump on to the said platform, he stopped dead on his tracks. He could only see a huge crowd of people and an occasional policeman on the place where he had left the bag. Kelo decamped faster than one could utter "Jack Robinson" to seek solace in the bottle he had left behind.

Sudhir was sitting on a bench, crestfallen. His mutton korma and coconut laddus were something which could not be forgotten easily. But he could do nothing about it. Suddenly a spark hit his not so bright brain. He should let the police know about it. With resolute steps he walked over to the Railway Police Outpost.

The second officer Chaubey was irate. Just as he was preparing for an afternoon nap, he was alerted by his superior office Khan who was going out leaving him in charge. Sudhir entered the Outpost at this juncture.

"Sir," wailed Sudhir. "My bag has been stolen!"

"What makes you shout? I am not deaf!" said Chaubey.

"Sir, my bag has been stolen." whispered Sudhir.

"Speak up, will you? Come here. I'll need all the details."

By the time Sudhir had finished speaking, a faint snoring could be heard from Chaubey's side of the table. Sudhir sighed and sat back on his chair. He knew that the stakes were very high, so exasperation would lead him nowhere.

Chaubey's slumber was but short lived. The shrill trill of the telephone cut mercilessly through his veil of sweet dreams. Sleepily he grabbed the offending instrument and grunted into the mouthpiece like a hibernating bear in the dead of winter. But the voice coming in through the wires blew the sleepy threads in his brain away like a cobweb in a whirlwind. He rang the bell frantically. A constable jumped in and saluted.

"Ramdin, get everybody ready. The minister is coming in twenty minutes."

Poor Sudhir tried to remind the officer about his lost bag. But Chaubey waved him aside.

"Yes, yes, I have noted it all down. You come back after the minister has gone. If your bag has remained lost for so long, then it won't come to any harm if it remains lost for another hour." Sudhir came out of the room dejected.

The crowd around the unclaimed baggage had thinned out. Time is the best remedy for any emotional upheaval. So, with the passage of time, interest in the article in question had waned. Now, there were more policemen than onlookers. Sudhir saw the officer-in-charge out there talking to a large group of constables. He knew Mr. Khan by sight, so he thought that he would address his woes to the top brass around. But as he came up to the officer, something else drew his attention. It was his bag! And it was being guarded closely by a number of guardians of law! The elated Sudhir scampered up to the group of policemen and elbowing all aside, pounced upon his treasure. There was a spontaneous uproar as the policemen thought that the bag would explode in an instant and all of them, including Mr. Khan, dived for cover. When nothing happened Mr. Khan crept out from behind the bench where he had taken shelter and grabbed Sudhir's arm.

"Why did you take the bag?" he asked in his best interrogative tone. "Is it yours? Then how come it was here for so long? Where had you been? Who are you? Can you prove that it is your bag?" Sudhir was flabbergasted at the barrage of questions. The crowd began to gather once again.

"Sir," Sudhir almost began to weep. "This is indeed my own bag. I can prove it. I had lost it sir, and now it has come back to me."

"Can you prove that it is yours?"

"Yes sir. There are containers filled with mutton korma and coconut sweets."

The officer shooed all the curious onlookers away, dragged the terrified Sudhir into his office, locked the door and checked all contents of the bag himself. The mutton was indeed tasty, as were the sweets. No 'seizure list' was prepared as no case diary existed. Within a quarter of an hour all 'evidence' had been consumed by the men in khaki and Sudhir was happy that he had got his bag back. Only then did Mr. Khan ring up his higher authorities to report that the case was solved and the bomb squad was no longer needed, neither were the dogs of war.

The Minister arrived within the next twenty minutes. He was followed by a long retinue of personal assistants, security personnel, party workers, admirers and, of course, the media. He strode on to Platform number 1 with long, purposeful strides. On the platform, he came to a standstill with such suddenness that his retinue crashed into each other. He called for the O.C. of the Railway Police. Mr. Khan stepped up and saluted smartly.

"Mr. O.C., where is the piece of unclaimed luggage that is the talk of the town today? I would like to address the crowd there. And why is the bomb squad late? What action have you taken? I demand a written explanation. And arrange for a press conference for me on the spot on this issue alone." Tribedi turned back to the camera, gave a dazzling smile when he noticed that the camera was running and patted his already sleek hair in place.

"Sir, there's no issue. The case has been solved. The baggage has been claimed and taken away by the lawful claimant. The bomb squad has been called off. There is no crowd to address. And, sir, if you want a press conference..."

"No need." Tribedi flashed a million dollar smile. Then he drew Khan close to him, draped his arm over his shoulder in an avuncular fashion and turned to face the camera. "You see, what a fantastic officer we have here. Please give him a big hand, will you?" As everyone broke into a spate of clapping, he muttered from the corner of his mouth into Khan's ears, "I'll get you transferred to a remote area, you bastard!"

The long-overdue express was announced to be coming in on platform number 3. All hurried towards the overbridge and platform number 1 was almost deserted. Sudhir scampered over the steps with his overnighter slung over his shoulder and the empty gunny bag with its empty containers clutched in his left hand. The minister stepped into the V.I.P. Waiting Room. The Express train whooshed into platform number 3. A drunken song broke out from platform number 5.

The story has been previously published online in 'Your Story Club' in June 2012.

✦ ✦ ✦

2

The Outlaw's Love

Today Khandu will be released from jail. This may not be a piece of news important enough to merit the morning's headlines, but important for the people of Chandipur, nevertheless. The tea-stall dwellers had little else to talk about over the last few days. The bus stand was agog with suppressed excitement. Children ran out into the muddy street, at every pretext, to eagerly scan the northern horizon, for the main road through which Khandu would enter the village, ran along that direction. Bnuchi's mother had forgotten to add salt in her dal, as she was engrossed to hear to the exploits of Khandu, being related with a lot of fanfare and justified exaggeration, by Lebu's aunt. By midday Khandu, by the word of mouth, had become a sort of a local hero.

"Do you remember how I once spanked Khandu for stealing guavas from my tree?" Nripati removed the hubble-bubble from his mouth to ask. The smoke from the tobacco burning like Vesuvius in full eruption atop the age old contraption traversed the wrong way and Nripati, called Khuro or Uncle by all the villagers, young and old alike, choked over in a paroxysm of coughing.

"Arre Khuro, of course we remember," said Kelo, the tea-stall owner. Nripati had a sizable amount of money unpaid in his permanent account of credit at the stall and Kelo was not ready to take any chance at all.

"Khandu was an out and out rascal in his younger days, if you don't mind my saying so," added he. "Now he has outgrown it all, I dare say."

"Kelo, pass me your match box, will you? There's a good man." Moinuddin drew on his bidi with great fanfare. He was the local primary school teacher, known as 'Master' to all. "Don't speak so lightly of Khandu. He's a veritable hero now. Can't you see?"

"Huh! Hero! Don't give me, Master! A crook is a crook is a crook." Nripati added profoundly in between of bout of coughing.

"Whatever he is, he has never harmed any of our Chandipur people, has he?" asked Haren, the grocer, sipping his tea served scalding hot by Kelo. "He is our very own, and that's that." added he, blowing into his earthenware cup to make his tea cooler.

Khandu was no political bigwig. He was no satyagrahi, either. He was a common criminal – a muscle on hire, it can be said. Yet he was becoming a veritable hero in Chandipur. But this is not a slur upon the good name of the peace-loving, quaint, little village. The reason was that nothing ever happened here. When Mangala, the cow of Haradhan the tailor, had calved, it made headlines in the village. When Ranga Babu had brought the first transistor radio from town, half the village had gathered in his courtyard an hour before he came, merely to listen to the evening news. The battery operated radio was a tremendous hit in the village that had no contact with the concept of electrification, even though it was quite some time after Independence. It was not surprising that Khandu had created more than ripples in the placid waters of the village tank.

Khandu was a tough guy, though thin and wiry in appearance, the exact opposite of what a hired goon was supposed to look like. But he was in great demand by all patrons within a radius of thirty kilometres from Chandipur. The simple reason was that he was a magician with bombs. This art of bomb manufacture was given the status of a cottage industry by Khandu. He was an authority on the subject. No one could match his quality nor his speed at getting the job done.

Pari was an orphan. She was brought up by her maternal uncle, as her mother, who was abandoned by her husband when she was just three months pregnant, had died in the throes of childbirth. She had grown up to be a beautiful girl, and was well accomplished in all household chores, including sophisticated ones like sewing and embroidery. Fair and beautiful, she was a treat to the eyes of the village youth... Pari basked in the attention she received. But as luck would have it, none of the suitors appeared to touch her mind and heart before she met Khandu, the bomber

It was the month of August. The heat was oppressive and days sultry. Even then there was no dearth of gaiety in the villagers as it was the time of the village fair. A brand of folk songs, known as Bhado Gaan, was a very popular item in this fair. Khandu was a great connoisseur of music. He never missed any Bhado or Baul mela if he could. He loved the night long musical soirees a lot. At such a village fair, Khandu had sat enthralled with the beat of drums, when his survival instinct suddenly rang a thousand bells inside his head. He felt, though he was not very certain, that someone was looking at him. The hair on the back of his neck bristled like that of a ferocious canine and he turned his head around steadily, avoiding any jerky or abrupt movement. Then he saw her. A pair of dark, doelike eyes was gazing at him, appraising him, reaching out to him. He had seen Pari. Eyes locked, hearts reached out. The background music, the Bhado Gaan became inconsequential now.

The show was not over yet, but Khandu stood up. Tottering to maintain his balance in the tightly packed audience, he tiptoed out careful not to put his foot into the lap of some one. From the section reserved for women, another person too flitted out. Pari could hardly contain herself.

"I am Khandu." said Khandu, introducing himself eloquently.

"I know you. Who doesn't?" quipped Pari.

With these wonderful introductions they ambled along across the fairground. They marveled at the toy train, gawked at the high Ferris Wheel, laughed at the frolicking clowns, bit tentatively into the hot cutlets, smeared their mouths with candy floss, and in general enjoyed themselves silly. Spring reappeared in August.

By the time they found themselves back in this world, it was already quite late. The night was dark with only a wan sliver of the moon fighting a losing battle against the darkness. Pari and Khandu lived close to each other. So they matched steps on their way back home, holding each other's hand for moral support. On the way they had to cross a bamboo grove. The bamboos were standing erect and black, with their heads nodding knowingly in the gentle breeze. They seemed innocuous enough, but to the trained eyes of Pari, they were sinister. She was loaded up to her tonsils with local folklore and knew for certain that this was the place which teemed with ghosts on moonless nights. That there was an apology of a moon in the sky escaped her notice and she clutched at Khandu like a drowning girl clasping a straw.

"O Khanduda', I am scared." she declared in a tremulous voice.

"Why? Oh, the ghosts? Don't worry dear. They all know Khandu." came the intrepid reply.

Then as if to reassure her, he bent down. Even in the darkness his lips found hers with unerring accuracy. Pari regained her courage, but lost her heart.

Soon enough, Pari got further evidence about the heroism of her beau. The youngest son of Pari's neighbour was running high fever. There was no doctor within a radius of ten kilometers. Everyone had to rely on the acumen of Tarini Doctor, the local quack. But in this case, even Tarini had given up as all his medication had failed. The crowd of onlookers was visibly saddened, till someone had an immense brainwave.

"Call Bishwambhar." suggested someone from the back of the crowd.

Now, Bishwambhar Ojha was not a person to be trifled with. He had a towering reputation in the locality as a scourge for all ghosts, living or dead. He was a swarthy middle aged man, with a flowing jet black beard and shoulder length hair. A dhoti of blood-red silk was his only attire, with a red piece of cloth draped round his shoulders. His very appearance evoked awe. He was reputed to have a couple of ghosts as his servants and at around midnight he played chess with the king of ghosts himself. He was a man of few words and communicated mainly through grunts.

Bishwambhar came in with two assistants in tow. The onlookers looked at this emaciated duo with awe, totally convinced that these two were the two ghostly servants they had heard so much about. Bishwambhar gave a glance towards where the sick child lay swathed in blankets and declared that a hostile spirit had taken up residence in the body of the boy. As he laid down the tools of his trade, a grinning skull, a pair of long bones, an urn of incense, a broomstick and other necessities, he declared in a sepulchral tone.

"I shall invoke the denizens of the netherworld now. Only with the help of these strong spirits shall I be able to drive out the evil spirit that the boy is harbouring. But, beware! When those spirits respond to my call and come within me, I may go berserk! If at that time any queasy or ungodly person comes close to me, the spirits may attack him forthwith. And I can't guarantee what will happen then! All of you had better leave."

A few left, though. No one wished to be branded as 'queasy' or, worse still, 'ungodly'. Pari too, stayed put, crouching in one corner of the room. A hundred wild horses would have failed to drag her away from the rare spectacle. Bishwambhar scowled this way, then that and finally settled down to light up a small pyre on the floor, into which he dashed a handful of incense, filling the small, crowded room with white smoke and a sweet odour.

It was at this juncture, that Khandu entered the room. He had gone to Pari's place in search of her and on hearing that she was in her neighbour's place made a beeline to the room where she was cowering with other teenage girls of the neighbourhood.

Khandu was a worldly man. At a glance he understood what was happening. He may be a crook or an outlaw, but he could not stand these sorts of emotional blackmail by playing on people's superstition. He crouched down low in the front row of spectators. Unknown to all, before taking his seat, he had grasped a stick, about a couple of feet in length.

Bishwambhar uttered vicious sounding chants, absolutely unintelligible and began to whirl about like a tornado having a fit. His chants rose to a crescendo and he smashed his fist into the ample tummy of the local quack. The latter yelped and fled the scene. An exodus followed. Bishwambhar's red-rimmed eyes began searching for the next victim, as his spirit-sodden breath vouched for the fact that he was indeed loaded with spirits of the wrong kind. He eyed Khandu and advanced. Pari shrieked. Bishwambhar raised his right hand to strike the skeptic Khandu down, but Khandu was more than a match for him. He too whirled around and brought the stick smack against the temple of the man in red. Bishwambhar was out cold. Then before anyone could react Khandu jumped up, picked the sick boy up, threw him across his shoulder in a fireman's lift and scampered away. He was not to be seen for the next three days, nor was the boy with fever. It was after three days that both returned to the village. The boy, it appeared, was cured. Khandu had apparently shouldered the child and ran on to the main road. There he took a bus for the nearest town and got the boy admitted to a hospital. Pari was all the more proud of her beau.

That very evening Khandu went straight up to Pari's maternal uncle and asked for Pari's hand in marriage. Her uncle coughed, hawked, looked this way and that, held a closed door meeting with his wife, Pari's aunt, and finally gave his grudging consent. The grudge was not because Khandu was not a worthy groom. Neither was it because of their affection for Pari. The sole reason was that they were being deprived of the service of an unpaid domestic help. However, uncle had to bow down to the inevitable and the couple got married within three months. Pari's happiness knew no bounds.

They did not go for a honeymoon. But there was nothing strange in their not going. There were three strong reasons behind it. The first reason was that the concept was not very clear to them. The second was that, even if it had been clear, they could hardly afford it. The third reason was that their house was right at one end of the quaint little village with no one around to disturb them. So they had privacy, with their green, shrubs, trees, flowers, fruits and their crystal clear tank. In fact they had all that was needed to keep a young couple in bliss. They had each other for company and that was their honey and that was all the moon they needed.

Of course, they went to the nearest town quite often, just to let their hair down a bit. They relished the hot and sour *Puchkas* (pani puri) sold in the town square and the fish cutlet in the tiny restaurant with fishy odour. They went to the cinema hand in hand, and sat there looking into each other's eyes in the dark, rather than at the silver screen. They bought trinkets for Pari, like a few bangles and earrings, with a sari or two, for good measure, and sometimes a pair of sandals for Khandu. Over and above, they were truly happy with each other.

But Pari's happiness, unfortunately, proved to be somewhat paroxysmal, as Khandu had to go away quite often for professional reasons. Added to it were the frequent interactions with the guardians of law. All this made Khandu stay away from his wife, often for quite a stretch of time. This was the only put-downer in their otherwise lustrous love life. But one could not have all one wished for. They were quite happy with what they had.

Three years passed by in this way, but the couple was still childless. In a village this was a scandal. Tongues started wagging. The old women of the village blamed one or the other, for what they termed as 'sterility'. Wherever Pari went she faced wry comments and sometimes tirades to this effect. This was unpleasant. So, one night, lying still, huddling close to each other, tired after all amorous calisthenics, Pari could contain herself no longer and spilled out to Khandu what she had been hiding in her heart so long.

"Ramu's *maa* has a scalding tongue." said Pari.

"Why dear? What did she say?"

"She was asking for how long have we been married."

"That is none of her business. Everyone knows how long we have been married."

"Yes, that's true." Pari lay still for a long, long time.

"Isn't it time we plan to have children?"

"What? What?" Khandu had fallen asleep in the meantime.

"Oh, yes. Children. Yes, that's interesting." Light snores told Pari that Khandu had already fallen asleep. She too turned over to sleep, but sleep eluded her. She planned that she would take the matter up again in the morning.

It was mainly Pari's anxiety that goaded them to go to the town once again, but this time to seek medical help. The elderly doctor took their history, examined them, prescribed several tests, took a pinch of snuff, sneezed majestically and pronounced both of them to be perfectly healthy after studying the test results. What the poor General Practitioner missed was the fact was that Khandu generally missed the most fertile part of his wife's cycles due to his professional trips or escapades of daring.

Chandipur lay plumb in the centre of the area politically dominated by the opposition. The ruling party had their own mechanisms functioning like a well oiled machine, but the opposition was sometimes rusty and no match for the rulers. Khandu's services were, therefore, much in demand from the opposition. This was no problem, as such, for Khandu. He was satisfied professionally and was secure economically. Only once in his illustrious career was he apprehended by the long arm of the law.

Khandu was on his way to a client with about half a dozen of his finished products in a gunny bag. He was whistling as he walked as this was the last of the consignment and he expected that today he would be paid for his efforts. He was planning that on the way back, he would drop in at the confectioner's to get some sweets for Pari, who had a sweet tooth. But his reverie was cut short by the sudden appearance of an apparition in uniform.

"Let's see what you have there in your bag." demanded the policeman.

"Oh, it's nothing sir." replied Khandu with a toothy grin. "Only a few coconuts for my *pishima*."

"Coconuts? Are they? Well, let me have a coconut then."

Khandu was arrested and taken to the police station. His actual crime was a bit different from what the records showed. He was recorded as carrying bombs. This was physically found to be correct. But his real offence was that he did not have enough money on him to oil the palm of the constable who had caught him red-handed. Khandu was bundled unceremoniously into the lock-up and left there to contemplate the world from behind the bars, not that there was much to look at though, for the police station was old and decrepit, with a couple of tables and a few worn-out chairs and a couple of racks overflowing with old, forgotten files. The blackboard on the wall showed statistics of crime, but the figures were at least a decade old. Hours rolled by. Pari, in the meantime had begun to grow anxious and Khandu began to get anxious feeling that Pari must be getting anxious by now, when the elderly, black telephone rang. The officer-in-charge picked it up and began mumbling into the mouthpiece with a number of sly looks towards Khandu.

Tapanda was a resourceful man and very well connected. Though he belonged to the Opposition, he had a number of cronies in the ruling bench as well. Moreover, he was the local elected Member of the Legislature. In short, he was not to be trifled with and it was common knowledge that there was a strong possibility that a change of Government was in the offing. The police was just a tool in the hands of those who ruled. So, the officer-in-charge found it prudent to pay total heed to Tapanda when he called for his protégé's protection.

He was Khandu's chief patron and it was his party office where Khandu was taking his products. The phone call ensured Khandu's release in a trice, while the official report nestled cozily in the depths of a strategically placed waste paper basket, where all such trivia were thrown in.

That day, when Tapanda's interference had saved his skin, it was evening by the time Khandu reached home. Pari had overcome her anxiety to get her daily chores done. She had just completed the evening rituals of lighting a lamp at the altar of their household deity at the Tulsi shrub and was blowing her conch, when she was surprised by a pair of strong arms embracing her from behind. Khandu's close encounter with the law had made him all the more amorous. He rained kisses on the exposed neck of his dearest and turned her around. Pari was flushed and breathing heavily. She was feeling the familiar warmth and the welcome sweet wetness.

"Not here, you oaf!" she chided. Khandu laughed and carried her over to their bed-cum-living-cum-dining room and plumped her down on bed. At this juncture, someone called him from outside.

"Who is it?" Khandu was intensely displeased, and why should he not be?

"Tapanda has sent me with a new commission. Come on outside."

"Come back later." Khandu grunted his reply.

"Are you coming or not?" The intruder did not have any manners!

"Do you think that Tapanda had intervened just because he likes you handsome face? The elections are coming. A lot's going to happen."

Pari pushed him off the bed and motioned him silently to make himself presentable.

This was Khandu's life!

There was one thing Khandu was afraid of most, and that was the police. He was not afraid of any being, spirited or dispirited, but the men in uniform gave him the quakes. He was genuinely afraid of being apprehended and sent off to jail for a stretch, leaving behind his lovely wife alone, pining for him. Once it had happened, just after his marriage, the couple was sitting together, hand in hand, head to head, beside the tank behind their house. It was a full moon night. The air was balmy and fragrant. They were saying nothing to each other, but sitting in comfortable silence, watching the floating moon breaking up into thousand pieces of luster, as each ripple rolled over, when a headlight of a jeep lit up the scene and broke their reverie. Khandu was startled out of his wits. Out of reflex he jumped right into the water and swam away. Later it turned out that the vehicle was not a police jeep at all, but a jeep belonging to the Irrigation Department. Khandu had got wet all over for nothing and sneezed all through the night for his pains.

On another occasion, and this was before they were married, Khandu was sitting on the steps of his house in peace, mending his torn shirt. It was late in the evening and the light was failing. So, Khandu set his stitching tackle aside and stretched and started humming a latest Hindi love song. Dusk had set in. In all the households conch shells were being blown to welcome the evening. A faint perfume of incense was hanging over the whole village. All was quiet and serene, when Pocha, the youngster, came running in. "Police," he mouthed. He was out of breath from running a long distance. Khandu jumped up and in reflex ran away from where he sat. He vaulted over the low wall separating his house from that of Podi Pishi's and dived into the heap of straw kept in a corner of the compound after harvest time. He pulled bunches of straw down to cover his face and lay there absolutely still. Podi was a mild mannered elderly lady who lived alone next door. She was affectionately called Pishi or Aunt by all inhabitants of Chandipur, young and old alike.

It was fortunate that Khandu had escaped to where he was, for the police had indeed come to look for him. There had been some semi-political disturbance in the vicinity and a great number of bombs had been used by both sides. It was not totally political, because some land encroachment issues were involved. And true to form, the bombs used by both warring factions were of Khandu's manufacture and Khandu's name had come up in the police enquiry that followed. Hence, the raid today. But, even in their weirdest dreams the police would never have the idea that Khandu was hiding in the elderly Podi's house. So, Khandu felt that he would be safe from prying eyes.

From his hideout amongst the straw, Khandu could hear the crunch of heavy boots and gruff voices calling out his name. He also heard Pocha's voice answering some questions the police were asking. He prayed that Pocha had the fortitude of hiding the mended shirt and sewing things he had left behind on the steps. He was hard put to stop sneezing as a strand of errant straw tickled his left nostril. Then he dozed off.

When he awoke, the police appeared to have gone away and it was dark and quiet all around. He must have slept about four solid hours! Khandu felt an irresistible urge to evacuate his bladder, full to the point of bursting. But he had not kept Podi Pishi in mind.

Podi was out with a lamp doing her usual rounds of her grounds before locking up for the night when she noticed the straw heap quivering.

"Got you, now," muttered Podi under her breath. "You foul dog, every night you come to my straw heap to commit nuisance and befoul it all by your faeces! I got you today."

She grabbed a bamboo pole lying handy nearby and tip-toeing upto her quarry, whacked him soundly on his head with a resounding crack, even as Khandu was peeping through in preparation of beating a hasty retreat. The yelp that followed was human enough to make Podi drop her pole in amazement. The night's sojourn had earned Khandu a tender swelling on his head and a full belly, as Podi had compensated her slip-up by giving him a mouth-watering dinner.

Tapanda had summoned Khandu on a special mission. He was commissioned with a large order to be supplied with utmost secrecy and urgency. Khandu started to work at a feverish pace from dawn to dusk, while Tapanda's men came in at regular intervals to carry the goods away. Soon the last lot was done and it was near evening. Tapanda's man had said that he would be back in the morning to take away the last bagful. Khandu washed his hands and feet in contentment and hung the bag of goodies up on a nail, in his multipurpose room, well beyond the reach of his wife. Then he went out to Quddus Mian, of the neighbouring village, to buy a fat chicken. Tonight he was happy. He would show his wife how to cook a real delicacy.

Khandu hummed a toneless tune all the way to Quddus Mian's place and back. He had come to a momentous decision and was all the more happy for it. A few nights ago, Pari, with tears in her eyes, had begged him to change his vocation and he had willingly agreed. Later he had fixed up a respectable job for himself at the local grocer's shop. All the people in his village loved him. He had landed this job quite easily, though he would have been happier if the pay was better. But, never mind, one could not have all that one wished for. They would pull through.

A wonderful aroma pervaded the whole house and the neighbourhood as Khandu began to demonstrate his prowess of a different sort. Both he and his wife were crowded in the small kitchen. The spices were fried and Khandu released the marinated pieces of chicken one by one to be fried next. Both were happily smiling, not at the prospect of a sumptuous dinner, but at the closeness they were enjoying now. The old nail, which the bag was suspended from, gave way a little bit, unnoticed. Khandu poured a measure of water in the well fried chicken and spice, and covered it to boil. He loved his chicken tender. While the dinner was stewing, Khandu decided to while the time kissing his pretty wife. The old nail gave way further. The stew got hotter and so did the kissing couple when the nail gave way altogether. The bag dropped to the floor. The resultant bang was so loud and vicious that the whole wall and part of the tiled roof got blown away. Apart from Pari, Khandu had only his chicken and his kitchen he could call his own. A chunk of tile landed on Khandu's head and knocked him out cold.

This was the second time that the law had got better of Khandu. But this time no helping hand was there to bail him out. He got a year's imprisonment for all his troubles, which was soon cut down to half its length for good conduct. Pari was inconsolable in her grief at the prospect of facing the world alone. But she was a brave girl and knew that she would live through her ordeal.

But, whatever it was, Chandipur was not ungrateful. Khandu had given the inhabitants something to talk about after a long, long time. The villagers responded wholeheartedly. They knew how to look after their own. Willingly they took up the mantle of guardianship of Pari, who became a sort of celebrity on her own. Many times she had to relate to the womenfolk, the details of what had come to pass that fateful night and it all passed into the archives of local folklore. The elders of the village gathered together a bunch of volunteers and together, they rebuilt the portion of Khandu's house that had unfortunately got blown away on that fateful night. The grocer gave Pari all things she would require during the time Khandu was cooling his heels in jail and reassured her that the job will be Khandu's whenever he returned.

Khandu ducked out of the small gate on the main gateway of the District Jail, like a hero in a popular Hindi film. He emerged into the sunlight, yawned like a minister during a boring speech in the Assembly and stretched like the Hindi film hero he had seen in the dingy cinema hall in town. But unlike the hero, there was no garland-bearing follower waiting for him. Just Pari was there, waiting for him, with all smiles. Garlands and cheering followers were superfluous now. His Pari was there, he needed nothing else.

"You had enough?" asked Pari.

"Yes," replied Khandu, all smiles, as he embraced his darling, little wife.

"Then let's go home. It has been repaired. But now I want a gift from you."

"What gift?" Khandu was curious.

"I want a baby girl."

The story has been previously published online in 'Your Story Club' in June 2012.

+ + +

3

The Village Yatra

The village was agog with excitement. Durga Puja was knocking at the door and Kartik Puja was around the corner. While Durga Puja was the biggest festival in Bengal, Kartik Puja was the most popular festival in this village. So everyone was excited. The senior citizens gathered around the village tea-stall and ruminated about past glories of this festival during the days of the British, when the Pal zamindars held sway, the housewives compared their saris and ornaments and exchanged juicy tales about the amorous flings of the village youngsters, the younger girls talked to each other harbouring a secret wish that their husband would be someone like Kartik himself, the school going children engaged in mock war-sports, no doubt inspired by the exploits of Kartik, their younger brothers ran about in senseless excitement, regardless of their nakedness as they ran yelling "Durga Thakur, Kartik Thakur" at the top of their shrill voices. A huge crowd of benign onlookers, from every age group, men and women alike, thronged the Chandi Mandap every day, monitoring the hourly progress of the images being made by the village potter, helped by his quartet of able bodied sons. This work force was indeed needed, as there were several images to be made – not only of Mother Durga, or her children, Lakshmi, Saraswati, Kartik and Ganesh, along with their attending animals like the lion, the owl, the swan, the peacock or the rat, but also the villainous Mahishasur and the slain buffalo. This year the Mahishasur was made up to be an extremely powerful and muscular man, bearing an uncanny resemblance to Gnyanda, the confectioner's helper, who, in all his free time, was seen to be performing free-hand exercises or whirling the heavy iron mace about his head, to tone his body, which he always referred to as 'the temple'. But all said and done, the curiosity of the villagers was mainly sparked by the cordoned off area in a corner Ray Babu's courtyard, where, hidden from the prying eyes, Nepo, the youngest and the most talented son of Pocha, the village potter, was making the image of the village deity, Kartik. Speculations ran riot. Some said that this year it would be a 'Babu Kartik', or Kartik dressed as a nineteenth century Calcutta zamindar, while others said that it would be that of 'Raja Kartik', bedecked in the fineries of a medieval king. But all this was idle speculation, as no one knew for sure what was being done. All barbed queries to Nepo went unanswered with a smiling shake of the head and Nepo had no close confidant in the village. He was a teetotaller and a bachelor to boot, so there was no chance of his spilling the beans. The village belles, out of sheer spite, kept reciting the age old poem.

Dyadang dyadang dangla, Kartick Thakur hyangla.
Ekbar ashe Maa'yer songe, ekbar ashe ekla

(Kartick was the greedy one.
Once he comes with his mother, then again he comes alone)

Only the young and the somewhat older men appeared to be sober and seen to be busy planning for the great event with the seriousness of cabinet ministers before the Prime Minister's visit.

"Impossible!" thundered Ravi, the local tailor. "We all know that there's a cash crunch. But that doesn't mean that we have to forego festivities." Ravi was one of the bigger contributors to this Puja and his opinion counted.

"Of course not." said Bipin, the Panchayat member, taking out his snuff box.

Moloy raised his hand like a schoolboy seeking permission to speak. He was a young teacher at the village school, a representative of the young vanguards and a drama enthusiast. Every year, famous yatra teams from Calcutta, performed in the village during the Kartik Puja festivities. But this year, the near drought situation and the consequent failed crop had all but put an end to expensive ideas.

"Kaku," he said, addressing Bipin as 'uncle' out of respect for his age and social position, "I have an idea that would cut expenses and, at the same time bring about better involvement from our own folks."

All stirred, their interest having been aroused. The sudden eruptive sound of Bipin's king-sized sneeze made almost everyone jump.

"Bipinda, how many times have I asked you not to take snuff while the meeting is in progress?" A rhetoric question this, from Monohar, the President of the Joint Puja Committee, that Bipin responded to by blowing his nose in a huge once-white-now-brown handkerchief, with a sound like that of the blowing of a trumpet.

"Kaku, what I meant to suggest was that why don't we stage our own yatra?..." The rest of Moloy's suggestion was drowned by a flood of hullaballoo of voices, with each giving his own opinion on the subject at the top of his voice.

At long last the decision was made by this elite body that indeed, they would be performing their own yatra on the Kartik Puja night. A budget was drawn up. Avenues of financial aid were sought and Kanai, the village barber and a long time yatra enthusiast, was entrusted with the duties of writing a script, with all help from Moloy. Ravi, however, rounded off with a dire warning to Kanai.

"You have five days to complete the script. Abide by this instruction and all will be ok for you, or else..." Issuers of dire warnings generally left the last part of their last sentences unsaid, as they themselves were not sure of the consequences. But the time-frame was justified, as five days later was Mahalaya, an auspicious day by all accounts.

Mahalaya, however, came and went. From 4 a.m., bleary eyed villagers had sat glued to their radio sets, listening, like every year, with sleepy bewilderment to Chandipaath by the celebrated late Birendra Krishna Bhadra with his fellow singers. Later there was community bathing at the village tank with mantras dedicated to the forefathers and a sumptuous lunch to follow. But the organizers were at their wits end as the barber's shop was closed with a notice hanging from the lock saying that the shop was closed sine die. The organizers ran their hands over their five-day stubbles while Ravi fumed. All questions directed at Moloy went unanswered. Something was brewing! All were worried.

On the evening of the seventh day, while the organizing committee met, a figure was seen scampering along the main village street, almost like Archimedes. It was Kanai. While Archimedes had run naked from his bath, dripping water all over the place, shouting 'Eureka', Kanai, clad in his usual white ran with sweat dripping all over, shouting 'It is done' and brandishing a roll of foolscap papers in his right hand. All breathed a collective sigh of relief.

Rehearsals began the very next day. Kanai had, no doubt, written a very good script. It was known as "Kurukshetrer Gada" (the Mace of Kurukshetra) and was based on the *Mahabharat*. There were plenty of action sequences with the encounter of Bhim and Duryodhan at its climax. The young people were elated.

Every evening a crowd gathered at Roy babu's courtyard and with the image of the half finished Kartik as witness, they enacted the scenes and honed their acting skills. The night air reverberated with their war-cries and dialogues of valour. The people of the village, ordinary mortals, were banned from seeing the making of this earth-moving drama. But within a week the younger boys were seen running about reciting scene after scene they had learnt by heart as every bit of the dialogue was audible to the whole village during rehearsals. Nutu, the village confectioner, in the new found role of the motion master, insisted that the actors should put their hearts into acting from the word 'go' if they were to go anywhere with their acting. The orchestra, too, was well orchestrated, comprising of a harmonium, a clarinet, cymbals and a drum. The musicians were all local talents. However, all through the drama they played what seemed suspiciously like the same tune of the song "Aaji eshechhi, aaji eshechhi, eshechhi bondhu hey..." from D.L. Roy's all time super-duper hit, *Mewar Patan*. But no one was bothered. The orchestra was playing, and that was all they could ask for.

Kanai, as I said, had written a very good script. The only snag was that, in spite of being told to the contrary, he had included one female character, that of Draupadi, though in one scene only. Ravi, cast as Yudhishthir, the eldest of the Pandava brothers, had resisted vehemently, but was overruled by Moloy. The greatest supporter of Draupadi was Gnyada, the muscleman, who was supposed to be acting as the strongman Bhim. Draupadi's only scene was with Bhim, where she eggs him on to rip open the chest of Duhshason, to drink his blood and to bring some for anointing her hair. The scene was studded with sparkling dialogues from both and Gnyada was not going to give the scene up without a fight. So Draupadi stayed. Nepla, the young lad who repaired bicycles at Sadhu Khuro's workshop, was roped in to act as Draupadi. He was a nice lad, of fair complexion and lanky build, who could, with the proper make up and make-over in the proper places, could masquerade for a passably comely damsel. His only defects were that he was taller than any of the Pandava brothers, but that was of no consequence, and he had a hoarse sort of a voice and tobacco stained teeth. To take care of these shortcomings, Nutu, the motion master forbade him to smile and urged that he should speak, from now on, in a squeaky, high-pitched voice of a woman. This put a lot of strain on the voice box of the hapless youngster. But no one paid any heed to his pleas and for this all had to pay a hefty price, as would come to light later on.

Durga Puja came and went, with all its accompanying gaiety. But the attention of the entire village was focussed on to the Kartik Puja and the yatra. Rehearsals redoubled in effort and time as soon as Durga Puja was over. The actors began to put together tinsel, baubles and golden papers to be used for ornaments. Hard at work was Bhim, for he had to put together a whole golden club or mace, or whatever. Ultimately he came up with an ingenious idea. He found an old pillow at home. This he pierced with a thick stick. Then he tied the pillow to the stick tightly with strings. He then covered the whole thing with a piece of cloth. Then he wrapped golden paper closely and tightly over all of it. Whatever the finished product was, it did not resemble Bhim's mace, though it looked striking anyway. His adversary Duryodhan, and his competitor in real life muscle building, was Podo, a short form for Kalipada. He was the local grocer. He went straight to town and bought a toy club, made of golden plastic. It was light and small, no doubt, but it resembled a club all the way and he was happy. His only problem now, was that he detested the last scene when he was supposed to be walloped by Bhim. He had decided to rewrite the script to his own satisfaction. In his rewritten Mahabharat, Duryodhan would not br killed by Bhim, but Bhim, beaten black and blue would run for life. This, of course, was his closely guarded secret.

The image of Kartik had been installed in the Chandimandap. It was indeed a Raja Kartik, resplendent in his princely attire. But our actors had no time to feast their eyes upon the glories of this image. Only two days remained before D-Day.

Ravi, or Yudhisthir, as he preferred to be called these days, had a sore throat. His voice, too, had gone hoarse. This was the price to be paid for conducting rehearsals at the top of their voices. But it was nothing much. It would soon be set right with a cup of tea, laced with a liberal dose of ginger juice. So he traced his step towards the tea shop of Potla.

"Potla, get me hot tea with a dash of ginger." he ordered. The tea was served as desired. Ravi/Yudhishthir sipped it with intense relish, 'hawk'ing now and then to clear his clogged airway, occasionally humming a tune to test his voice. Just one day remained before this tired voice box was to be put to test.

"Potla re, two parts tea and one part juice of ginger," cried a hoarse voice. Startled, Ravi turned to see Gnyanda, still sporting his makeshift mace.

"You too, Bhim!" exclaimed Yudhishthir. Caesar had met his Brutus! But woe added upon woe.

"Potla, tea, ginger, half, half," someone croaked. Hebo the carpenter, was it? Playing the role of Arjun? Yes indeed! Ravi all but swooned. But wait, dear Yudhishthir, sir, more is yet to come!

But they did not have to wait for long. Soon the terrible twins of the village Jodu and Madhu – Nakul and Sahadev in the Yatra – turned up like a pair of bad pennies.

"Potla," they squeaked in unison, "one part tea and three parts ginger." They were almost inaudible, so they had to resort more to sign language rather than anything else.

A lanky youth ambled in with effeminate gait. It was Draupadi I mean, Nepla. He walked straight up to Potla and handed him a slip of paper. On it was written in bold letters, "ALL GINGER, NO TEA".

The drama, I mean yatra, should have been a fiasco. Strangly, it was not. It was indeed a grand success, with the audience rolling in laughter at the temporary aphasia of Draupadi. But Bhim rose to great heights at this scene. He started the scene like this:

"I understand my dearest, you have cried yourself hoarse with all the sufferings you had. I am aware that you want to say..." This he followed with Draupadi's entire dialogue. He carried on like this throughout the scene and that part ended to everyone's satisfaction. Well maybe everyone's except Draupadi's. But that could hardly be helped. But poor Bhim! He knew not what awaited him in the last scene!

Duryadhan alias Podo, had made up his mind. He was not going to die. When the battle of maces began, he gave the audience its money's worth. Well, not money's worth, exactly, for all had entered free, but the spectators felt that it was time well spent! Bhim and Duryadhan battled on and on. Duryadhan received countless blows on his thighs, each of which was supposed to knock him out. But he stood there, steadfast like the Colossus of Rhodes and refused to give in. The motion master, yelled from the background, "fall, fall," but all these mundane instructions fell on deaf ears. It seemed as if Bhim's last day had come. The yatra has a few inherent disadvantages and the absence of curtains is one of them. So the show went on and on. Bhim's mace burst at the seams and cotton flew all around like snowflakes. But Duryadhan's plastic club was no match for the unencumbered stick Bhim held in his hand. It was sent flying. Bhim was fighting for his life now. Sensing deep trouble, Bipin, as Krishna, came up and stood between the warring duo, starting to sing the national anthem at the top of his voice. The musicians were delighted as they knew this tune. It was a relief from playing the *Mewar Patan* tune for three hours at a stretch. All the participants scrambled up to the stage to take part and the audience stood up singing lustily. Thus ended the great yatra of the decade, and everybody went home intensely happy.

✦ ✦ ✦

4

A Summer Wedding

Samiran took his kurta off and threw it out to a corner of the room in disgust. It was soaked in sweat. His vest was soaked too, but he could not remove it for propriety's sake. After all he was a guest here and had to maintain some sort of decorum. He lay on his back and stared at the ceiling. Sleep eluded him, not that it was essential, but a good siesta after a sumptuous lunch was always welcome. The ceiling proudly displayed a hook to which a fan should have been hung. Only this illusory fan was missing. This room, or rather, hall, was a newer addition to his host's house and was far from complete as yet. The walls needed a coat of paint. The ceiling needed a fan and the floor too was incomplete. Their host had allotted this unfurnished and unadorned room to them only to ensure their privacy. Samiran sighed and turned on his side. An ineffective table fan swung in the far corner, albeit in utter languor, emitting a peculiar sort of groan that rose and fell with the swing. What was it doing there anyway? thought Samiran. It gave out more sound than breeze.

Samiran and his friends were all young medics who had just completed their housejobs after graduating from the same college. They had come to a remote village in Midnapur district on the occasion of the marriage of their bosom friend and colleague, Sandipan. This was the ancestral home of Sandipan and his parents still resided here. It was from this house that the groom's party, called *barjatri* in these parts and *barati* in northern and western India, would go with the groom to the bride's village. They were to start this evening. The marriage was scheduled for midnight, which, the elderly Brahmins had jointly declared, was the most auspicious hour. Sandipan's marriage was a relief for them all. At last they would be free from hearing the sordid details of the courtship of that moron, which they had been bombarded with over the years. Tanima had been a distant relation of Sandipan, the second cousin of his maternal aunt twice removed or something like that. Their whirlwind romance had begun a few years ago when she had got herself enrolled in Jadavpur University as a student of Comparative Literature. Now that chapter at least was nearing its end, to the relief of all concerned.

That fateful morning they had started from Howrah Station in a local train for Contai. Contai was a big town with more bicycles and cycle rickshaws on the road than men. There they had taken a van rickshaw which would take them to Sandipan's village. Samiran had no idea that these vehicles ferried passengers as well. He had always thought that these were used to transport goods. Anyway, all of them sat cross legged on the floor of the vehicle clutching at whatever they could for dear life, as they swayed and bumped their way on to the village, some seven kilometres away. It was a memorable and painful journey. On arrival they had been given a welcome fit for kings and after lunch, they had been escorted to their present quarters. Sandipan's father was apologetic at the non availability of a ceiling fan, but our intrepid heroes had brushed all apologies away with heroic nonchalance and Samiran was paying the price now.

Samiran turned the other way. Four out of the six beds in the improvised dormitory were occupied by his friends. Anwar was sleeping on his back, resembling a supine and comatose walrus, with his handle bar moustache. Sudip lay on his side, curled up like a brooding foetus. The snores of Debu reverberated in the confines of the rooms like a diesel engine negotiating a Simla tunnel and Gautam was muttering obscenities in his sleep. In disgust Samiran sat up on his bed and threw his slipper at the snoring giant, Debu, which merely bounced off his bulk. The sleeping beauty did not stir nor stop snoring. Samiran reached for his pack of cigarettes. How on earth could these guys sleep like this in this goddamned heat and humidity! His eyes, roving aimlessly around the room, fell on the open doorway and stopped. A pair of large, ugly feet came into his line of vision, being anointed with the red, liquid *alta*. Who could it be? Only women of the house adorn their beautiful feet with this stuff! But he had seen no women yet with such a pair of Neanderthaloid feet! He stood up and tiptoed out. The groom, Sandipan was lying on his back, getting his feet anointed, in accordance with the local custom. God! It was hilarious! Samiran ran back into the room and poked his room mates awake inviting them to see the comic scene. But the buffoons all rolled over to resume sleeping with a vengeance. So Samiran had only one option left. He went outside, strode across the body of the grinning ape, Sandipan, and went in search of a cup of tea. Only tea would rouse the clones of Rip Van Winkle out of their slumber.

After tea the friends assembled near the pond at the back of the house to enjoy a quiet smoke. They were now fully dressed, complete with perfume and stuff, for their onward journey. They had not been able to ferret out the details of their travails ahead, but were mentally prepared to face all ordeals. Even then they were not prepared for the spectacle that unfolded before them, causing them to choke on their cigarette smoke. A procession was coming up the village street. That the procession comprised wholly of children, was not the cause of their consternation, but the leading object was. It was a palanquin!

"A palanquin!" exclaimed Anwar. "Can they still be found these days?"

"Apparently they can be." observed Samiran.

"Don't tell me that the oaf Sandipan is going to travel in a palanquin to get married! He'll take about a month to reach anywhere in that!" Debu was aghast.

Debu's apprehensions were unfounded. The procession led by the groom's palanquin, followed by his closest friends, the band party belting out Hindi songs, his relatives and the village urchins legged it up to the main road about two kilometres away. There, a bus was waiting to carry them further, looking resplendent, covered by garlands of bright yellow and orange marigold. A loudspeaker at the top of the bus blared out Bengali love songs. The band party was stationed on the roof of the bus. They wanted to give all concerned their money's worth by continuing to regale them with Hindi film numbers. It was sheer torture to anyone's auditory faculties.

With the musical cacophony unabated, the bus meandered past the town of Contai to reach the broad and expansive River Haldi. It had become dark by this time and the river looked ominous and black. A number of country boats were tied to the bank, to ferry the *Barjatris* across. The hearts of the city bred friends quaked at the prospect of crossing over, but there was no way out. Gautam missed his footing, fell into the river and got his trousers thoroughly soaked. But it was all part of the game and nobody minded anything, except Gautam himself. Everybody piled in to the boats, including the band party, and their voyage began. In the dark Samiran could not make out whether they were moving backward or forward. Sandipan kept standing in the boat like a twentieth century Columbus, grabbing the main mast, in eager anticipation.

All good things come to an end and all bad things too. After some time the crossover was complete and our heroes heaved a collective sigh of relief. It appeared that none of them knew swimming.

The ghat where they landed was well lit-up by sodium vapour lamps. A big reception team awaited their arrival and soon all of them were gorging on an assortment of sweets of different shapes, sizes, flavours and colours. A bus, decorated like the last one, waited for them on the street. All got in but that the band party was nowhere to be seen. Minutes ticked by and the waiting *Barjatris* got restive. It would be a shame if the auspicious moment was allowed to slip by. A few of the locals fanned out to search the neighbourhood. An hour went by. Now all began to get worried. Had their boat capsized while crossing? But, surely at such an event the drowning men would have called for help! After a further wait of a quarter of an hour, a chorus of singing voices with jumbled consonants and slippery vowels could be heard, followed by a number of tottering persons staggering up to the bus. The band party had, like a lot of homing pigeons, ambled straight and unerringly, even in the dark, up to a local country liquor shop about three hundred odd yards downstream and had get totally soused.

It was close to midnight when we entered the bride's village on foot. The groom, of course, was not allowed to walk with the commoners and was transported once again like a piece of worthless, though antique, item in a palanquin. Porters with gas light showed us the way. In this village, any village I mean, midnight is not the time for loitering about. It is the hour of the drunk, the burglar or the alley cat. Even the dogs pull down the shutters and sleep the sleep of the just. But the good villagers of this drowsy little village proved to be a tolerant lot. Not only did they tolerate the band and dazzling gas lights, but also they were good enough to crowd their doorways peering with bleary eyes to get a glimpse of the specimen of drowsy humanity swaying dreamily in the palanquin.

It was well nigh one at night when Samiran and others got the opportunity of sitting for dinner. They were on their alert, as Sandipan, before the wedding rituals began, had beckoned Samiran to whisper urgently in his ears a few words of warning.

"Be on your alert during dinner time. In these parts, the girls from the bride's side are notorious for their pranks and practical jokes on the groom's friends."

So they were now eating with great caution. One never knew what could happen. Maybe the appetising Mutton curry will be laced with a lot of chilly powder so as to make a tiger run for dear life! Or there maybe stone chips in the *rosogolla* (rasgulla)! But none of them were ready for what came to pass.

The first missile was fired when Anwar was chewing a particularly juicy drumstick. He was savouring the fare with eyes shut, when, splat! It landed right at the back of Anwar's head. It was nothing lethal, of course, but sticky and annoying. The well directed rosogolla hit its target with unerring accuracy and burst showering its shrapnel, in the form of its syrup and white fragments of itself, upon Gautam and Debu. Volley followed volley. The groom's friends were all smeared with this sweet onslaught from head to toe. Samiran had turned to locate the assailant. He froze. A pair of doe like eyes made him captive. The blue sari clad beauty gave him a coy smile. Samiran was so smitten that he failed to notice her lethal left hand. She was a lefty, by the way. Splat! The syrupy ball landed in between his eyes with mathematical precision. Samiran lost his heart and his face too, in the bargain.

She was Anima, the younger sister of the bride Tanima. She was the star of the attacking side. Her prowess raised peals of laughter from the ranks of girl brigade. Samiran felt the infatuation ebb and his hackles rise. He turned to call Debu, but the Don of the students' hostel was nowhere to be seen. Later they discovered him cowering under the dinner table.

The whole group was enraged. Bathing at two in the night, and that too immediately after dinner, is an ordeal in the best of circumstances, even though it was summer time. They decided that enough was enough; they would be off as soon as day broke.

Dawn found our heroes slinking out of the back door, with their bags and things. But a rude jolt awaited them. Standing in front of the door, barring their way, was an Amazon with a long staff in her hand.

"No one leaves the house of Nandis without having breakfast." growled Anima. "Leaving by the back door, are you? I'll crack the skull of any boy or man or whatever, who tries to leave."

Our heroes came back sheepishly, though mentally gnashing their teeth. Anima, in the span of just a few hours had made a number of sworn enemies.

The full moon cast its magical beam through the open window to light up the countenance of the bride. It was the following summer. With her doe like eyes the bride followed every movement of her groom. She simply adored him. The groom came up to her and drew her into a close embrace. The rest, as they say, was history. The lights still flashed in the illuminated gate lighting up the words "Samiran weds Anima."

The story has been previously published online in 'Your Story Club' in June 2012 and was selected as Story of the Month.

✦ ✦ ✦

5

Who Goes There?

"Who goes there?" The cry rang out every now and again, breaking the silence of the night. It did not bother the villagers of Chandipur anymore. They had got used to it. At the most, they turned over to the other side and went back to sleep. Or, if they were elderly and chronic insomniacs, like Potol Kaka, they got up from bed, went outside, relieved their aching bladders, came back arranging their dhotis and slipped back into bed, trying to get some sleep before the sun rose.

We used to call him "Khuro" or uncle – plain and simple Khuro. No name, no surname, just Khuro he was and Khuro he remained. Gradually this name engulfed all Chandipur and people of all age and description began calling him "Khuro". In his heyday, Khuro was the village watchman, patrolling the streets with his lantern and stick, crying out at intervals, "Who goes there?" It did not matter whether anyone was really going anywhere or not, what mattered was that those would-be miscreants who prowled about at night heard him and knew at once that Chandipur was awake and alert.

During his solo nocturnal vigil, he was always accompanied by his dog, a mongrel, but a really handsome creature, black as night itself, with a white mark on his forehead. Khuro fondly used to call him "Kaloo", because of his colour. Kaloo was intensely devoted to him, followed him everywhere he went. And there was every reason for it, as he had been picked up by Khuro after his mother, for some unknown reasons, had abandoned him to his fate when he was small pup. Khuro had brought him home, nurtured him, had fussed over him, and in fact did everything that a parent did. It thus stands to reason that the villagers said that Kaloo was the only family that Khuro ever had. No one, not even the oldest among the villagers, could ever recall Khuro having any family of his own. But one day, Kaloo died. Everyone has to die after his life span is over, but poor Kaloo's had been cut short by a bullock cart, that had run him over. Khuro was devastated. At that time I was away from the village, so I cannot say exactly what had transpired, but I heard that since that fateful day of Kaloo's sad demise, Khuro had stopped talking to anyone. All day long he used to sit on his veranda, mumbling, as if talking to Kaloo. He stopped his nightly patrolling, but all night long he used to sit at his doorstep, occasionally crying out, "Who goes there?" All said that poor Khuro had lost his mind. An old lady from the neighbourhood came over to give him food everyday. All his life, Khuro had taken care of the village. Now the villagers took turns in taking care of him. This arrangement continued, for Khuro remained as he was, silent and morose.

I was returning to my village after a long, long time. By this time, I had completed my education in Calcutta and secured a good job in a multinational firm. Now I had a family, a flat and a car of my own. I knew not what prompted me to return to my roots, at least for once, and here I was. My last remaining relative in the village, my uncle, had passed away a couple of years ago. So I had written to the caretaker who looked after the house, saying that I would be coming over on such and such a date. I sincerely hoped that the house, one of the few in the village built of bricks and mortar, would be spic and span.

It was quite late, when I entered Chandipur. The streets were all deserted and the village, bathed in the silvery light of the full moon, looked like a haunted village. A couple of years ago, the River Ajay had flooded the village badly. Since then nothing had been the same. The village was still trying to come to terms with the changing environment. More *pucca* (strong) brick buildings had started coming up, but the village wore a lost and forlorn look. Most of the youngsters had left home to search for a better future in the big cities and towns. Only the very young and the elderly remained. The recent spate of political violence in the vicinity had not helped either. Even though I could make out electric poles here and there and could hear the faint murmur of a television news reader, I could not help thinking to myself, "Is my village dying?"

I was walking along the deserted street immersed in my thoughts, when a sudden call startled me and broke my steps. "Who goes there?" Khuro! He was still alive! Although I knew perfectly well that Khuro's call was meant for no one, I could not tear myself away. I retraced my steps towards his house. There he was, sitting by himself near his open door. I went over and sat down near him, putting my overnight bag down beside me.

"Khuro," I gently called. Khuro tried to focus his near sightless eyes upon me.

"Who is it?" He asked, peering to make out my features in the light of the moon.

"It is me, Khuro, Sukhen. Harenbabu's grandson."

"Ah, Harenbabu's grandson! You have come home at last? But, my dear boy, why are you so late?" I had no answer to his question. Silence reigned supreme. After, what seemed to be an interminable time, Khuro sighed and said.

"You have grown so big, dear boy."

"Yes, Khuro. But I'll always remain that Sukhen to you."

"Always?"

"Yes, Khuro, always." Again Khuro fell silent.

"Khuro, how are you these days?"

"Who, me? I am alright, my son. By the way, didn't Kaloo see you come in? He has always been so fond of you...comes running in wagging his tail whenever he sees you coming...but where is he now?"

"Don't worry, Khuro, he had seen me come and had met me as usual." What else could I say? I could not break a broken heart twice.

"Ah! Then it's alright. So tell me child, how are all at home? Your father? Your uncle?" All were gone Khuro, all of them. But I did not have the heart to tell him that. So I lied.

"All are well Khuro, all of them."

"You remember son, the night I played Duryodhan against your uncle's Bhim? Ah, what an actor your uncle was! And what a yatra! There will never be another one like it ever again."

"Yes, Khuro. I remember it still. You were awarded a medal, weren't you?"

"Yes, you remember it then." His unseeing eyes were focussed on the bamboo grove that crowded in over the nearby pond.

I knew what he was seeing. He was seeing the arena of the yatra, dazzling with gas-lights, so lovingly called day lights by all, as they illuminated the environs like daylight. He was seeing hundreds of people sitting in the audience rooting for him. He was hearing the concert playing, the tune of the clarinet, the wail of the violin, the beat of the drum, the clash of cymbals. He was waiting for the exact note that would be his cue and the gong of the bell that would signal the beginning of the scene. He used to cut an impressive figure, with a height of more than six feet and a physique to match, resplendent in regal garb. With a booming voice and a clear enunciation, he used to play Duryadhan to life. In his last scene he used to fall on the stage, with his golden mace dropping from his hand in his encounter with my uncle as Bhim and looking at Tinukaka as Yudhisthir, he would deliver his last dialogue in his sonorous voice, "I go now. I go Yudhisthir. You are the victor! Enjoy your throne and with your brothers, rule over a kingdom where none but the carrion eating jackals, vultures and ghouls hold sway!"...And applause...thundering applause!

"Khuro, I'll go now. I'll be back tomorrow. Why don't you take some rest?"

"Rest, dear boy? How can I take rest? The village needs to be patrolled! But you go now. It is getting late. Kaloo, hey Kaloo, why don't you see Dada home?" He called out for

Kaloo, mentally seeing him emerge from behind the house, wagging his black tail.

The encounter with Khuro had made me sad beyond measure. Oh! How I missed old Kaloo too! After dinner, served by the caretaker, Charan, I walked up the stairs to the terrace. The air was pleasantly cool and fragrant with the perfume of some night blooming flowers. The pond at the back of our house was still there, the water deep and black at night. The moon shone on it, shattering into myriads of pieces, floating away along the ripples, to the banks. The bamboo trees on the opposite side nodded as if saying, "Welcome back, son."

Suddenly there was some commotion the street on the far side of our house. A lot of people were running about, calling out to each other. I could make out nothing, so I ran down the stairs. I met Charan midway. He was coming up in haste, bounding over two steps at a time. He had been running and was out of breath.

"Dada," said he, panting, "Khuro is dead." It was Charan who had found him lying where he sat, dead.

Almost the whole village had assembled in front of Khuro's place. All loved him dearly. Nikhil was there. He was a childhood friend of mine. He looked up as he saw me. His eyes, in the light of the lantern, seemed to be bloodshot.

"Sukhen, you have come?"

The pall bearers picked up the cot which served as the bier on their shoulders. I was amongst them. The strong perfume of cheap incense made me dizzy. The bunch of white flowers tied to the four feet of the cot, swayed in time with our movements. With a muted chant of Hari's name we matched our steps for the Burning Ghat, by the side of the river.

The path wound ahead, white in the moonlight. The village lay behind us, silently mourning the demise of Khuro. Far away, across the paddy fields, a tall figure seemed to be striding away, stick in hand. A lone black dog ran along behind him, wagging his tail. My vision dimmed, as my eyes brimmed over. The bamboo trees lining the path, nodded their heads in unison. Wind rustled through their leaves, as if sighing and whispering, "Who goes there?"

✦ ✦ ✦

6

In His Own Coin

It was a sweltering day in the middle of summer. There was not even a faint whiff of breeze. The mercury shot up every day. Nobody was sure how hot it would get. The asphalt on the roads was melting into a glue pot. Even the 'clang' of the tram's bell seemed to be tired and languid. Calcutta, it was not known as Kolkata then, was panting and sweating.

The three friends were exhausted and irritable in the heat. They were sitting in the shade of the college portico, having ice cream with abstract dejection, utterly bored with life. All were in the first year class of Physics Honours, in a premier institution in Central Calcutta. Today their class had been called off suddenly due to the sudden and sad demise of a long serving peon of the college and they had heaps of time to spare.

"God! Life is so boring!" Binay said flicking his stick off towards a dustbin and, as expected, missing it altogether.

"Let's do something, yaar, something horrendously thrilling." quipped Anwar.

"Like what? Tell me." Binay challenged.

"Let's go over to the Coffee House." Anwar suggested.

"No way, I don't have enough money. Spent all my pocket money last weekend."

"This comes from trying to court the wrong type of girl. Look at me. I never make this mistake. I simply say 'Open Seasame' and the girls' purses open up for me." Ajay stretched and said.

"Aha, is that so? Then where are your girls gone now?" asked Binay.

"Home. All gone home." Ajay replied.

"Come, let's go home too. This heat is getting on my nerves." Anwar stood up brushing the seat of his trousers.

"You want Auntie to call the doctor?" Ajay asked innocently.

"By the way, has anyone seen Shankar around?" Binay asked. The others shook their heads.

Precisely, at that very moment, an Ambassador car, of a sickly green hue, was seen to be nosing through the college gate. It spluttered, all but stopped, then coughed a bit, let go a whole lot of obnoxious black fumes from its rear end and inched over to the portico. A sweaty dark face peeped out of the driver's side window and yelled, "Hey guys!"

"Shankar!" all cried out in unison. "Where had you been since morning?"

Shankar parked the vehicle, his father's, got out and banged the door shut.

"Dad's not in town. So I thought I'll take old dustbin for a stroll."

"B-but do you have a license?" queried Binay the sceptic.

"What do you take me for? Now, who's coming for a spin?" There was a mad scramble to get into the car. At last they had something to do.

"Hey, you guys listen, stop!" Someone was calling out from the canteen. They saw Hari, a couple of years senior striding up to them. They got out of their car. Hari, euphemistically called Dirty Harry by his class mates, was a bit out of breath from the unaccustomed exercise.

"Yes, Harida," asked Shankar, "What can we do for you?"

"Care to go for a flick?" asked the portly youth, physically a far cry from the one he was named after. "*Enter the Dragon* has released at the New Empire, you know, *Enter the Dragon*? Bruce Lee? Kung-fu?"

"Yes, yes." all of them cried in unison.

"If you wanna go, I've four tickets to spare. You can have them at cost price." Hari was magnanimity personified. Shankar reached out and snatched the tickets.

"Thanks a ton, Harida, will pay you tomorrow."

"Mind it is for the noon show. Show begins in half an hour's time."

"No problem. Harida." Anwar turned to reply. "We have got our own car. Be there in a jiffy, with heaps of time to spare. Isn't it, Shankar?" Shankar scratched his chin, cast a dubious look at his car and nodded in reluctant agreement.

But the car had ideas of its own. It simply refused to start. No matter how much Shankar tried, it just stayed put. At last, all three of them, leaving Shankar at the wheel, lent their hands, literally, and the car spluttered back to life, but not before the expense of litres of sweat, tons of energy and ten minutes of their precious time had been spent.

"Don't worry guys; we'll be there in time. See, they show a whole lot of newsreels and advertisements before the film begins. Don't they?" said Shankar the optimist.

"Yes." said Ajay, occupying the front left seat. "Only if this blasted thing doesn't stop midway. I'll be damned if I push the car again!" he declared with a vengeance.

"Arre, don't worry yaar! That happens only if I stop. I won't. So no hassle."

By the look of things, the picture was brightening every minute. The oppressive summer heat had kept most of the people indoors. There were few cars around and even the automated traffic lights backed them up, showing them the green signal. The car zoomed merrily along, well, as merrily as an octogenarian with wheezing bronchitis can. All was going well till they reached the Bowbazar crossing. Then Fate caught up with them.

It was not Shankar's fault. He was not supposed to let the car stop, come what may. Added to it was the fact that they had only ten minutes to spare, before show began. But the decisive factors were that there was no car in the vicinity of the crossing, and the two traffic constables were jawing in the shade. When there was an automated signalling system around, why had Calcutta Police posted two useless constables there, only God, or the Police Commissioner could say. Anyway, Shankar had looked first this way, then that, and then he had jumped the red. The "phew" of the police whistle sounded like thunderclap!

Shankar was unfazed. He gently eased the car over across the deserted crossing and parked the vehicle. Then asking his friends to stay put and not to worry, he ambled across to where the policemen had stationed themselves, fishing into his hip pocket for his wallet. Now, the times that I am speaking about, were not too healthy for the bribe aspiring constables. The notorious Emergency Period had just got over and the hangover was still there. Any policeman caught in the act of taking money was heavily penalized. Therefore, when the two men were seen to be violently shaking their heads as Shankar approached them, it was perfectly understandable. They were seen to be shaking their heads, then nodding, shaking them again and finally gesturing onwards. Shankar was next seen crossing the road, to walk over to a betel shop round the corner. He said something to the shop owner. The boys tensely were observing the scene from within the car, saw the betel shop owner gesturing towards the policemen and putting up two fingers. One of the constables violently nodded and the shop owner raised his right hand signifying that the deal was understood and clinched. Shankar sauntered over, back to the car, with a smug look, and started the engine. Peculiarly enough, this time the car responded with alacrity. As he accelerated, Shankar began laughing. He guffawed so much that tears streamed down his cheeks. The steering wheel wobbled, scaring an unsuspecting pedestrian out of his wits. After a while he sobered down, but made such an announcement that his friends were sure that he had been touched by the sun.

"Today I shall stand the movie and the snacks." he declared.

Apparently Shankar had made a kill. His friends made him tell the story before they entered the darkened hall. They were as such late for the show, and, well, in for a penny, in for a pound!

The policemen had a tacit arrangement with the betel shop owner, that the latter would carry out all illicit financial transactions on their behalf and would hold on to the funds for a future settling of accounts. Shankar had gone straight up to this financial wizard and had told him officiously that the policemen were asking for twenty rupees to be handed over to him for some obscure services rendered. The shop owner had asked with the help of sign language whether he was to give this sum to the young man. But, as luck would have it, the policemen had misread the signs. The two raised fingers signalled for twenty rupees. The policemen had ordered him to take the sum; the shop owner thought that he had been instructed to hand over the sum. So, Shankar came back twenty rupees richer.

When they entered the hall, the action had already begun, with Bruce Lee's sister, on screen, of course, kicking all nonsense out of a villainous rogue. But none of the guys minded at all.

✦ ✦ ✦

7

The Amateur Vet

Bashir Ahmed is a wondrous guy. I mean wondrous, not wonderful. The more I see him, the more I am filled with awe and wonder. He is just a ward boy in my nursing home, who works in the operation theatre, but in practice he is my indispensible assistant. I know not what his duty hours are, or when he takes some time off, for whenever I enter the O.T. area, I find him there, moving about, straightening this furniture, sterilizing those instruments, going through the next day's O.T. schedule, in a word always as busy as the proverbial bee. He is a cheerful guy too. Always smiling at his job, he loves his jokes. A prankster to the core, his colleagues are ever alert lest be play practical joke on them. He spins a good yarn too, and amongst his brilliantly narrated tales, it is often hard to discern which is fact and fiction too. He has a good voice, he often sings to himself, whenever he is free. Apart from all this, I have noticed that over the years he has developed a clinical acumen beyond compare. An immensely likable character, he has gradually developed into a person whom I cannot do without.

He comes from a village some sixty odd kilometres away from my town and from what I have heard, he is well respected out there, not for the fact that he works in the town, but because he is a very good 'doctor', both for men and animals, who can perform a minor surgery or two on his own. He goes home every month and generally stays put over the weekend. Apparently he remains busy for these days too. He tends to patients, gives his opinion regarding ailments and performs a number of minor operations. Well, 'minor' is the term he used when recounting his tales to me. But from what I heard from his peers, his surgical prowess is seen as stupendous by the people of his village, who do not care whether these operations are technically minor or major. Many families are known to arrange for the ritual circumcision of the boys in the families as per Bashir Ahmed's schedule and convenience.

A couple of months ago he came back from a stint in his village bubbling over with exuberance and joy. He did not need much coaxing to come out with another of his stories.

It was near evening when Bashir reached home. The first house he crossed at the fringe of his village was that of Khudu Mian, the celebrated and venerated butcher of the village. Khudu was a busy man. He catered not only to the needs of his own village, but to those of about five other villages in the close vicinity as well. Bashir found him sitting in front of his house whetting a huge knife, and humming away to his heart's content.

"You seem to be well pleased with life Khudu *Chacha*." Bashir called out.

"Arre, Bashir, when did you drop in? Nice to see you, boy."

"Just arrived, Chacha. But tell me, such a huge knife... where is the *dawat* (party)?"

"*Arre, na re baba*. There's no *dawat*." said Khudu."It is a sad, sad tale." But his expression belied his statement.

Bashir could never resist a good story, so he moved over and sat beside Khudu.

"What is it, Chacha?" he asked.

Bashir sighed and put his knife down.

"You know Moin Sheikh, I suppose?" Bashir nodded. "Well, he is in a soup." Khudu added dramatically, tickling Bashir's inquisitiveness to no end. Moin was well known in the village. He was a well to do farmer who owned sizable plots of arable land and had a two storeyed building in the village, though in public he professed to be a poor farmer. All the members of his family had the coveted BPL card, BPL standing for Below Poverty Line. If you are a supporter of the political party in power, you can move from APL to BPL at the drop of a hat.

"You have seen his beautiful black she-goat, I suppose. She is in labour."

"Who? The goat?" asked Bashir, totally confused.

"Yes. Since yesterday. But she hasn't delivered till now. So Moin is asking me to put the goat out of misery. Apparently he loves the goat as his very own."

Bashir perked up. This was directly in his purview. He had been assisting in obstetric cases for quite some time now. Obstructed labour was something he really understood. He stood up and tentatively brushed his backside.

"What's up, young man?" asked Khudu.

"Nothing. I have got to go now. See you later Chacha." With this he strode towards Moin's house, steeled in his resolution.

"Hey," called Khudu. "That's not the way to your home! Where are you off to?" cried Khudu.

"Chacha, I'll tell you all later." Bashir replied from afar. He had started running.

Though made of mud and tiles, Moin's house was something to look at. It was a double walled house. The outer wall enclosed the whole perimeter, and sheltered the cow sheds too. There were four cows tied up side by side with their noses shoved in mangers, enjoying a grand repast of fodder, on the left hand side of the main entrance. On the other side the shed became more spacious, accommodating a pair of white bullocks as huge as Shiva's Nandi, and a pair of buffaloes as black and as towering as two ominous rain clouds. The buffaloes eyed Bashir with intense dislike and suspicion. With a quaking heart Bashir ran into the sanctuary of the main house enclosed within the inner walls. In the courtyard he stood looking this way and that. No one could be seen.

"Chachi, o Chachi," called Bashir.

"*Ke re*?" asked a gruff voice.

"O, Moin Chacha? Salam Chacha. It's me, Bashir."

"O, Bashir? Come in beta." the disembodied voice of Moin responded. Soon the master of the house came into view. He had completed the evening prayers and had been giving the morning's newspaper a once over.

"Chacha, heard that you had been having a lot of trouble with the birthing of your goat?"

"Oh yes, son." said Moin, sadly. He pointed towards his left and said, "There she is, the poor soul."

"Can I take a look, Chacha?" asked Bashir.

"Take a look, son. But I think that she's past any human help. I've asked Khudu to come in the evening."

"I know Chacha. I've met Khudu Chacha on my way and heard it all from him."

Beyond the house were a kitchen garden and a pond, one of the four that Moin possessed, of course none was in his own name. A crowd of curious onlookers and labourers were gathered by the side of the pond where the poor goat lay in a sorry state. Bashir went up to her, examined her and sent a lad forthwith to his own house to bring his bag of essential articles.

"And what did you do next?" I asked.

"Why sir? I did a caesarean section, of course." came the prompt reply.

Bashir anaesthetized the goat using the same injectable anaesthetic agent, Ketamine, that he had seen his Anaesthetist didi using in short procedures at the nursing home and as to the dosage, he was smart enough to go by body weight. The goat could hardly be heavier than the small boy he had seen being anaesthetized only the week before.

"And then?" I was very anxious about the well being of his patient.

"The kids, sir, were dead unfortunately."

"No, no." I insisted. "What about the goat?"

"Khudu Chacha had his evening off, sir. He lost his case. He got really annoyed with me."

"And Moin?"

"He was overjoyed, sir. The very next day he threw a party to celebrate the occasion, with rice and fish curry. I was invited, sir. And from what he told me, he was thinking about giving up mutton and red meat of all sorts because his doctor from town had forbidden him to take them."

Next month Bashir went home again. I met him on the day of his return. He was busy taking the drums out of the sterilizing machine.

"Bashir." I called.

"Sir." the guy materialized as soon as I called. This boy was a veritable Genii of the Lamp!

"How's your patient?" I asked.

"Grazing, sir."

✦ ✦ ✦

8

Chandi Charan's Pet Dragon

Thunder crashed and forked tongues of lightning ripped the heavens apart. The rains will come later. Now, gusty winds blew debris about in a flurry, and ruffled the crowns of the tall trees out there in the garden. A window banged somewhere. Chandi was a light sleeper. The banging window awakened him instantly. He glanced at the alarm clock kept on his bedside table. The luminous hands told him that it was 2.25 a.m. An unearthly hour, this. Chandi grunted in displeasure and swung his legs off his bed. Fishing blindly about for his slippers with his feet, he took a long draught of water from the bottle he kept at hand. The entire house was dark. Thunder pealed once again and the window shutter banged in the drawing room. Chandi stood up and groped his way to the switchboard. He fiddled with the switches but to no avail. The power had presumably been cut due to the inclement weather. Chandi cursed under his breath and stumbled across to the drawing room to shut the offending window.

Chandi Charan Chaki was a poet. Don't ask me why, but just let it stand that he was a poet. But being a poet could hardly ensure his staying alive in this world, so he worked as a Bengali teacher at a local school, all the while teaching children and young adults but conjuring poems, rhymes and couplets in his mind, all day long. He was reputed to be a good teacher. When he taught *Meghnad Badh Kabya*, a Bengali classic, his characters seemed to come to life. He was a magician with words. Often he scribbled out poems on the most unlikely pieces of stationery available, like the back of the laundry bill or a blank space at the bottom of a doctor's prescription. Once the local general practitioner had turned him out of his chamber just because he had 'defiled' his precious prescription with scribbled pieces of poetic inspiration. The doctor had misunderstood his misplaced genius. But, in spite of being such a gifted poet, he was still searching for a publisher. He had his own band of a handful of friends and admirers who declared that he was one of the greatest poets of this millennium, but they were biased and their opinion hardly counted. He had, of late, been rejected by five publishers in a row. The last one had said that there was a great potential in him and why did he not start writing some poetry instead! Then what had he been doing so long? This uncalled for advice made Chandi go through his poems once again, though wading through the hundreds of unpublished works of literature was an arduous task indeed! After this he concluded that whatever he had written was indeed poetry. This exemplified the typical feature of this unfortunate nation, that the wrong man was invariably at the wrong post. The person, who was supposed to be the poetry editor, had no idea about poetry whatsoever.

Called C-cube at school by friend and foe alike, Chandi was a long surviving bachelor, staying alone in his ancestral house in the small town in Burdwan district. Of course, Raghu was there as a domestic help, taking care of everything in the frugal household. But the poor man had suffered from an acute attack of appendicitis and had to be hospitalized a couple of days ago, and was successfully operated upon. So, now Chandi was home alone, without a guardian, pending Raghu's return.

Even though Chandi lived alone and was a bachelor, he had no vice to speak of, except a wee bit of indulgence of a spirited kind. He loved his drink and indulging in a glass or two during the quiet, boring evenings went down well with him. He had few friends, and so all his drinkings were solitary in the serene privacy of his own home.

It had started raining. Half of the drawing room was already awash with the blasts of rain being carried in though an open window by the strong wind that was still blowing about unabated. Chandi rushed in to shut the offending window, getting half drenched himself, in the process. As he was struggling with the shutters, lightning flashed with the crash of thunder. The brilliant flash lit up the entire garden and Chandi noticed that someone was standing underneath the huge mango tree, gazing up towards the open window. The figure looked familiar, although Chandi could not be very sure who it was. In the darkness Chandi stood rooted to the spot. Rain had drenched him thoroughly by now. But he had to find out whether he had really seen someone standing there, or it was a hallucination of some sort. The lightning flashed once again. But this time there was no one to be seen out there. Perhaps the flashes of lightning had played some sort of a trick with him. Anyway, the whole thing appeared to be spooky. Chandi shivered as he pulled the shutters close. He suppressed a sneeze hoping that he would not catch the death of a cold and went for a thorough drying from head to foot and a change of clothes.

A strange, very low hum greeted him as he entered his bedroom. Chandi looked about him, perplexed. He could not locate the source of the sound. Then his eyes fell on his bedside table. The crocodile or turtle egg or whatever it was, that he had carelessly been using as a paperweight, was humming like a mobile phone on vibration mode, and was emitting a very faint luminescence. It seemed as if it was coming to life. A pale pinkish orange glow seemed to be coming from within it. Chandi tentatively touched the surface of the ball, but immediately drew his hand back, as if electrocuted. It had felt warm. He reached out once again. He could not resist it. It was as if the thing was drawing him to it like some strange magnet. This time he placed his entire palm over its surface. The warmth coursed through his whole arm and appeared to flood through his being. All chill and malaise disappeared. Chandi drew his hand back and gazed at the object, as if in a trance. In a while, however, the humming ceased and the glow went off. The thing had been sitting here over the last three days. But this was the first occasion when it had behaved strangely. What was it? Was it something extra-terrestrial? Chandi had seen many sci-fi movies and was conversant with the concept of aliens. Or, perhaps it was the egg of a T. Rex, as in Jurassic Park. Whatever it was, it was strange! Chandi lay back on his bed, his eyes never leaving the ball for an instant. He knew that something momentous was going to happen. But it never did, not through the whole night, in spite of Chandi's sleepless vigil. It was a good thing that the next day was a Sunday.

Exactly three days back, Chandi had encountered the 'thing' for the first time. It was at around one in the afternoon and Chandi had the next period 'off'. So he headed towards the teachers' room, planning to take a quick dig into his lunch box and scan over the morning newspaper once again. Muted voices were coming from behind the closed doors of the room. Chandi pushed the door gently and peered in. A number of his colleagues were crowded at one end of the long table, inspecting something very closely. Seeing Chandi, Buddhadev, the English teacher, called him over and asked him to shut the door as he entered. They were inspecting a round object, more like an ellipse than round, pearly white in colour. They had set it on the centre of the table. Chandi had never seen anything like it earlier.

"Can you guess what it could be?" asked Mahim, the Arts teacher.

"No idea. What is it? An egg?" Chandi ventured to ask in return.

Prakash, the Physics teacher, lifted the thing up and weighed it mentally.

"It is quite heavy. Whatever it is, it is of high specific gravity," said he.

Mahesh, the Bio wizard, was sitting there, going through the newspaper. He peeped from behind the paper and peered at the object once again.

"It is nothing but an egg, I would say. A crocodile's egg. But the feel is like a turtle's egg, though." He, with his Master's in Zoology, was the only qualified person around. It emerged that about a week ago, Mahim had gone to Kathmandu, for a visit. There he had befriended a Tibetan monk who had given him this object as a gift, saying that it would bring him luck. The monk had not divulged the nature of this thing, but had pushed it into his hand and was gone. But now, Mahim's wife was dead against having such an unidentified object in the house, even though it was a gift, a token of goodwill. Mahim was a man riddled with superstitions of all kinds. He was averse to throwing it away, fearing that any such slight will bring him bad luck, nor could he keep it in his house, given the opposition he had faced on the home front.

"Chandi, my friend," said Mahim in a voice dripping with honey, "You are my true friend. Will you please help me in this matter?" Chandi had a bad feeling about this affair.

"No way!" said he.

"Please, Chandi, just keep this thing with you only for a few days, till the storm on my domestic front blows over. I promise that I'll take it back when things cool down."

"But, why me?" Chandi asked.

"Because you are the master of your own destiny."

Chandi looked at the strange object. He felt a peculiar affinity towards it. He reached out to take it in his hands.

"Ok, I'll keep it. But remember, it is only a temporary arrangement."

Mahim agreed heartily.

It was a grey and faceless Sunday. The sky was overcast and the day, sultry. It was near about ten in the morning when Chandi awoke. On waking, the first thing that came to his mind was the series of events that had taken place the previous night. With a bit of apprehension he eyed the egg on his table.

But it was sitting there inert and lifeless. Chandi thought that all the weird happenings were nothing but figments of a fevered imagination. His weekend noggin must have been a bit more than judicious.

Chandi spent the whole day surfing. By lunch time, he had become a veritable authority on the subject of reptilian eggs. He studied all sorts of reptiles, starting from turtles and tortoises, moving on to crocodiles and alligators, and ending up with snakes of all kinds. Next he was planning to start off with paleontological eggs. But, even though he had become an amateur 'eggologist', he was still clueless regarding the egg in his possession. After a sumptuous lunch of his favourite Sunday dishes, rice and mutton curry, he felt that he should first take a nap, before resuming his forays into reptile-land.

When a horde of marauding mosquitoes woke him up it was close to evening. Half awake, he called for Raghu to bring him a cup of tea, only to remember that his aide-de-camp was in hospital, nursing what remained of his gut, after amputation of his appendix. So, he yawned and mentally prepared himself for a sojourn in the kitchen. At this juncture his eyes fell on the table and he almost had a heart attack. All his efforts since morning had been brought to naught. The egg was not there. He searched all possible places, but it had simply vanished in thin air. He rang Mahim up to inform him of the loss, but found no solace from that quarter too. Dejected, he sat down in front of his TV with a cup of tea. The programme being shown was that of a Chinese New Year, with crackers, paper lanterns and paper dragons. It bored him stiff and he began to jump channels, only to bore himself further. A fat gecko clucked on the far wall.

That night sleep came to him in a strange, interrupted manner. He woke up several times in the night, always feeling that someone was calling out his name. But when he got out of his bed he could find nothing extraordinary in the whole house. A peep through the window failed to reveal anything unusual in the garden either.

School next day was a mundane, run-of-the-mill affair. One class followed the next till the final bell rang. But Chandi had been jittery to such an extent that several of his colleagues had enquired about his health. Mahim had even gone to the extent of giving him some unsolicited advice. He felt that Chandi should marry and settle down in life. "What is life, without a wife?" He had asked. Chandi had grimaced in chagrin and moved off.

It was no better in the evening. The same old TV and the same sort of boring programmes... Lastly he settled for Fashion TV and goggled at semi-nude beauties to soothe his frayed nerves.

His sleep was interrupted again, this time at around one. He felt that someone was prowling about in the drawing room. Chandi got out of his bed and tiptoed over to the closed door of the drawing room. There was indeed a faint whisper coming from within. It was ill-defined though, but very much there. Stealthily Chandi opened the door. He was, by nature, an intrepid sort of a personality, but what he saw nearly caused him to faint.

A strange sort of a creature was moving about in the room. Sniffing around, rather. It was like no creature he had seen earlier. It looked like a giant reptile, yet it was not a crocodile. The thing looked vaguely familiar, but he could not place it. In the faint wash of moonlight coming in from the open window, it appeared shadowy and floating about. Chandi pinched himself to ascertain whether he was asleep or awake. Although he had been as silent as a church mouse, the creature seemed to sense his presence out there, and turned. A pair of eyes, glowing like burning embers transfixed him. Chandi felt that his end was near and braced himself for the possible attack. But, no! No attack came! The creature stood on its hind legs, as easily as a biped and beckoned to him with his right paw. Chandi entered the room and drew the door shut. Then came another shock. The creature spoke to him...well, not spoke, exactly, for no sound emerged. But it communicated with him straight inside his head. Unspoken words reverberated within his cranium making a weird sense. The creature was telling him that he could switch the light on, if he so desired, for humans could not see very well in the dark. Chandi acquiesced. As the room was flooded with light, the creature gestured to him to take a seat, while it seated itself on the arm chair at the far end of the room. Chandi sat down and began his appraisal of the strange phenomenon sitting smugly in front of him.

The creature was almost as tall as Chandi when it stood on its hind legs. It was muscular and appeared to be very powerful. Its skin was of a dark green colour, almost like that of moss that can be seen on the hills. Its eyes were luminescent with the colour changing from emerald to fiery ruby. It had a longish snout which accounted for the fact that initially Chandi had confused it with a crocodile. A pair of wide nostrils surmounted the apparently cruel mouth, set with vicious looking sharp teeth. Occasionally the nostrils emitted what appeared to be, thin tendrils of smoke. A long row of spines ran along its spine to end at the tip of a rather longish tail. Was it...was it...

"Yes, you've made the right guess. I'm indeed a dragon," said, or rather communicated the creature. "But you shouldn't be afraid of me. My appearance might be fearsome, yet you need not have any fear concerning me. On the other hand it is I who shall protect you from all misfortunes."

"But how come, I mean, why, I mean..." Chandi was eloquence personified.

"How am I here? Why I thought that you had guessed that too! I have hatched from the egg that you had so faithfully guarded over these last few days. I know no mother, nor any father. You are the only one whom I know. You are my family. And we dragons have a weakness. We take carc of our own.

"Now, let me get another thing straight. You must be wondering how I can talk to you. This, my dear man, is called non-verbal communication at its finest level. But enough is enough! It is getting late, go back to sleep. I shall be keeping vigil. So don't worry."

The next day was the last working day, before the school closed down for the summer vacation. Chandi was back home a bit earlier than expected. His dragon was waiting for him. Chandi freshened up and had his meal. The dragon sat and watched, like a mother hen looking after her brood.

"Won't you eat something?" asked Chandi. He was perturbed at the dragon just sitting there and following every single movement of his hand, without batting an eyelid, well, it did not have one to bat, anyway.

"I don't eat all this." replied the dragon. "I am a carnivore."

"Then what am I? Do you thing I am having this chicken stew because I am a herbivore?"

"No, not that. I am a carnivore of a different kind. I feed on minds, memories and intellect."

Chandi sat staring at the dragon. He was simply astounded, nay, flabbergasted at this strange reply.

"Don't worry," reassured the dragon. "You do not figure on my menu card."

Chandi resumed his eating in silence. Then suddenly a thought struck him.

"By the way, dragon, I hope you won't mind if I ask you this question. Are you a male or a female? I mean, a he or she?"

The dragon let out such a lord guffaw, that a couple of pigeons, planning amorous adventures on the rooftop, flew off in abject terror.

"Of course I am a male! I would have made passes at you last night, had I been a female!"

The picture of a she-dragon cuddling upto him in bed was so horrendous that Chandi choked on his food.

The dragon now looked at the clock on the wall. He appeared to have something in mind.

"Enough of this useless talk. It is time for my scheduled stint of good deed. Tell me, what I can do for you today. I have taken it up on myself to do you one good deed every day."

Chandi sat back. Actually he needed nothing apart from getting some of his poems published. The dragon, as usual, read his mind.

"It will be done, mate," said he. "Soon your book of poems will be published. Mark my words."

By the time Chandi dropped off to sleep, he had clean forgotten about this promise. Therefore, the phone call from the poetry editor, who had once advised him to write poetry, was a matter of mild surprise for him. The editor asked him to drop by at his office at around noon. He was to carry an assorted collection of his poems with him, for these poems would be published very soon. Chandi, was naturally, elated. Then a thought struck him. Did the dragon have anything to do with this windfall? The more he thought about it, the more his suspicion grew. He went over to the drawing room.

The dragon was lounging in the easy chair, sitting with his legs crossed, humming the time of a very popular Hindi film song tune from the seventies, tapping his left foot in time with the rhythm.

"Hey," Chandi accosted him. "Where did you learn that tune from?"

"Shhh..." the dragon silenced him. "It is being played in a house about four kilometres away. Can't you hear it? But, how can you? You are a mere human."

"You mean..." Chandi spluttered. The dragon shut him up, putting a finger on his lips, or what passed as lips on his reptilian countenance. After the song had apparently ended, he sat up and looked at Chandi.

"Were you saying something?" he asked.

"Yes, I was." Chandi said with indignation. "The poetry editor rang up." The dragon smiled, exposing his sharp teeth and fangs.

"I know," said he. "I know all about that. I had visited him last night."

"You mean, you went to his place?" Chandi was incredulous.

"Well, not exactly to his place, but I visited his mind. I can reach out to any person in his dreams, or better still, in his nightmares. I told him what I wanted. He gave in. A cowardly person! Didn't want to face consequences."

The next evening saw them arguing vehemently. Another publisher had rung up asking for more poems for publication. He had promised to publish all Chandi could dish out. Chandi was flummoxed. He was agitated too. He did not wish this sort of favour, accrued through dubious means.

They were arguing loudly, so much so that neither had seen the old hand Raghu enter the room. He coughed.

"Arre Raghu, you are back! You ok now? Recovered fully?" Chandi's happiness knew no bounds.

"Yes dada," said Raghu. He called Chandi, 'dada' or elder brother. "But who are you talking to?"

Chandi looked at the dragon in bewilderment. The latter shook his head. Then Chandi understood that the dragon was invisible to Raghu.

"Me? Talking? Are you mad, Raghu?"

Now, Raghu got really scared. He had been standing there unnoticed for quite some time and had seen for himself that Chandi was talking to someone. He resolved to have a talk with his master's friend Mahimbabu. He could hardly stand by and see Chandi becoming mad.

The Psychiatrist, Dr. Some, was a good, soft spoken person, with rather prominent front teeth. He smiled like a benevolent patriarch when Chandi insisted that he was neither seeing any vision, nor was he suffering from hallucinations of the auditory kind. He kept on smiling when he scribbled out the names of a few medicines for Chandi. Chandi had a good mind to knock those Bugs Bunny teeth out. Only a stern look from the dragon restrained him.

Things went on like this for a fortnight or so. When the dragon asked him about his medicines, whether he was taking them or not, Chandi usually replied, "Why should I? I am not mad, am I?" The dragon smiled that alligator-smile of his. When Raghu asked him the same question, he replied with a smile, "Of course I am taking them. I am much better now. Am I not?" Raghu smiled. He was happy too. Little did he know that the dragon was always around and was watchful as ever. The other day, Chandi met Mahim in the market place. They had lost touch lately as the vacation had started. Mahim knew it all though as he was instrumental in taking Chandi to the psychiatrist.

"Hello friend, how are you?"

"Oh, I'm fine!"

"Seen any more visions of late?"

"None whatsoever. Your doctor knows his business." Chandi replied, with a wink at the dragon, standing unseen over the right shoulder of the short statured Mahim.

At the first follow-up visit of Chandi to his doctor, Dr. Some, however, smelt that something was fishy. It was a case of drug defauling. He insisted that Chandi take the same medicines as before, but, taking no chance, he entrusted Raghu with the responsibility of giving him the medicines and Raghu was to ensure that Chandi took them all. Chandi had no way out now. He had to take all medicines given. Nowadays he slept too much, no doubt due to the action of the drugs. He missed the dragon very much. As he was asleep for the better part of the day, possibly the dragon was considerate enough not to disturb him. Over the last ten days or so, they had not met at all. In the meantime the final proof came from the publisher. The next month his first anthology of poems would hit the stands.

Dr. Some was elated. Examination and cross-examination of Chandi had revealed that he was now cured of his ailment.

"Now I'll give you these medicines for a month. You see I have taken off most of the drugs. By the end of next month I'll stop the drugs altogether, for you'll be totally cured of any hallucination by then. Both visual and auditory kinds. But, even now you are not having any vision or hallucinations, are you?"

"Oh no, doctor, I am perfectly free from hallucinations now," said Chandi with a smile, with the merest flicker of a glance towards the corner chair. The dragon smiled too and winked as he gave Chandi the 'thumbs up'.

✦ ✦ ✦

9

The Last Bus

The pain was excruciating! Been that way for quite a few days now. It started generally in the centre of the chest, right where he had a red birth mark next to his left nipple and then it spread all over. Must be the heart! He should have married when there was still time and energy to nurture a family. But now it was too late. His hair had started turning grey. Then came the bifocals and now this nuisance, the pain in his heart. He would rather have preferred a heartache of a romantic kind, but that was not to be. He thought as he trudged home all by himself, not sure whether he would get a bus or taxi at this unearthly hour. He should have gone home straight from the doctor's chamber. But no! He had to dally! It began to drizzle. Not a steady downpour, but a drizzle nevertheless. By the time he reached the main road, he would be thoroughly wet. Not even a single rickshaw was in sight. Slowly the rain turned into a downpour.

The doctor took a pretty long time in examining him thoroughly. He looked at his last ECG, the X-ray, then banged his chest with fingers, closely listened to his heart, made him cough and listened, made him sit up and listened, made him lie back again, took out a fresh ECG, hemmed and finally pronounced that nothing was wrong with him. As he was the last patient for the day, the doctor could afford to take all time in the world.

So, nothing was wrong with him. That was what the doctor had said and the doctor knew best as he was a fully qualified cardiologist to boot. When he had declared that nothing had happened to him, there could be no scope for any doubt. But he, as a patient, was very finicky. At the bottom of the prescription he had noticed that the doctor had scribbled something in the strange scribbling sort of handwriting that only a drugstore person could decipher. It began with a question mark. The doctor said that he had noted there that the case could be that of an 'Unstable Angina' and had prescribed a Treadmill and a Halter Test, or whatever they were supposed to mean. But he was not going to die today. So the tests could wait.

The tests could wait, but his friend could not. As he was coming out of the doctor's chamber, he was accosted by an old friend. That the man was a failed poet, was immaterial. He could not help it, neither could his friend. But, today, the friend had reasons to celebrate. His poem has been published in a little known journal. So he dragged him over to a large bar behind the tram depot that specialized in country liquor. The night had suddenly become young and the environs mellow.

The unearthly hour, together with the rain, had served to keep all vehicles away. Luckily he had the foresight of asking the serving girl at the bar for a piece of waterproof wrapping. The doctor's prescription was safe. Otherwise the 'unstable' something would have been transformed into paper pulp!

After waiting for five minutes or so, he gave up the idea of getting any transport and began to walk, shoulders hunched against the driving rain. Suddenly, out of nowhere a bus came up, headlights blazing, with the conductor calling out, "Last bus, last bus." Without even asking the destination, he clambered aboard and plumped into the nearest window seat and looked about him. It appeared that he had the bus all to himself. He bought his ticket from the conductor and settled down on into his seat, thoroughly miserable.

The bus sped on and on without stopping anywhere. There was no reason for it to stop, because there was no other passenger and the wet roads were deserted. Rain slashed against the window pane. The world seemed dark, mysterious and lost. A few streaks of light flashed by denoting that the whole city was not asleep.

He must have dozed off. Outside it was pitch dark. Rain was still battering the window pane. He tried to see the time, but his watch had stopped. He took his cell phone out of his pocket, but that too was not working. The rain had soaked it thoroughly and damaged it altogether. He turned in his seat and found the conductor huddled in a seat near the door, apparently dozing too.

"Haven't we reached?" he asked the conductor.

"Almost there." came a guttural reply.

He settled down again to wait for a while, till at long last, the bell clanged. The bus slowed and he stood up.

"Mind your step, the footboard is all wet," the conductor cautioned in a sepulchral tone. "Drat this rain!"

"Don't worry, I'll manage." He replied, getting down from the bus with cautious steps. No matter how much he had tried, he had not been able to make out the features of the conductor. It was as if a handful of the night's darkness had been smeared over his face, rendering all features indecipherable. This was strange, he thought.

The bus started again the bell was rung twice as soon as he alighted and sped away, spraying muddy water from the wet road all over him. He jumped back to avoid being splashed, as if he could get any further wet!

The bus sped away, along with its blazing headlights, plunging the area in total darkness. It was still drizzling. It was so dark that all sense of direction was lost. The overcast night sky precluded the possibility of any starlight to show him the way. It was as if the directions, north, south, east and west had been were put in to a mixer-grinder and whirred at a speed of three hundred rpm. But he could hardly stand rooted there till dawn. It would look very foolish! So, he started walking and made his way forward. The only information at the back of his mind that got him going was that the lane which led to his house, started off at right angles to the main road, towards the left from where he stood. After proceeding confidently for a few paces, he stopped, unsure of himself. The ground felt strangely muddy and slippery, but his lane was a metaled road. There must have been some mistake somewhere. The drizzle stopped at that moment and a glimmer of light came to his eyes.

It felt like a hallucination at first. He felt rather than saw the light. But, it was something to latch on to. So he went forward, cautiously putting one foot in front of the other. Soon the vague illusion of light grew to become a real flare. A bonfire was burning merrily in a clearing in the surrounding jungle.

All the while he had been traversing a jungle track! But where did this jungle come from? Something was far too weird! He moved up ahead, stealthily this time, taking care not to make any noise. Crickets chirped to break the wall of silence.

A number of men sat around the bonfire. They seemed to be villagers. Their bare torsos gleamed in the light of the bonfire. All wore dhotis, bound tight about their waists, up to their knees. Their foreheads were adorned by vermillion tilaks. At one end of the clearing was an awesome image of the goddess Kali, resplendent with a garland of human heads and a skirt of severed limbs. An assortment of gleaming steel weapons was piled up near the image. About eight to ten feet away from the image was a *harikath*, a sacrificial altar, complete with two raised limbs of timber and besmeared with old blood. Nearby, a young man was lying, apparently asleep, but gagged and bound. Dacoits! Thought he. About to perform a human sacrifice! But did these things happen in real life? He had read about such things in story books when he was a child. A roar sounded from far away to break the silence. A tiger? Where was he? Somewhere in the Sunderbans? The dacoits laughed as they drank. He crouched further down in the shrubbery as he watched the scene in front of him, mesmerized. Mosquitoes buzzed all around him enjoying their free banquet.

Maybe an hour had passed, he had no means of knowing, when one by one the dacoits fell asleep, soused by the drinks that they had so liberally consumed. He waited for some more time. Soon their sonorous snores filled the night air. They had left no sentries. He now broke cover and crept out towards the sleeping, gagged and bound man. He could not very well sit here idly and smugly watch a human sacrifice taking place! He had to set the man free.

Very cautiously he inched up to the sleeping victim. It was a relief to find that his own clothes had dried up by now; in fact they felt so dry that he was astounded. It seemed as if they had never been wet! But further surprise awaited him. As he was creeping towards the gagged and bound man, his bare knee got scratched by a thorn of some jungle shrub. It hurt, but bare knees! He was wearing jeans, to the best of his knowledge, which had been utterly soaked! But now, in the light from the bonfire, he could see that he was wearing a short dhoti and tough leather sandals. Along with the jeans, his sneakers appeared to have vanished! He was absolutely bowled over at this turn of events. What was happening!

However, he did not get enough time to reflect over the strange things that were taking place, for one of the dacoits turned to his side, mumbling to himself in a drunken stupor. He froze in his tracks. If the dacoit opened his eyes, he would be done for. But soon, the dacoit began snoring and he inched closer over to where the gagged man lay.

As he reached the bound man, he moved over to his far side. Then hurriedly touching his head to the ground in the direction of the image asking pardon for stealing the goddess' quarry, he began to untie the knots securing the man's wrist and legs. Only when he was done, he undid the gag. The victim was a young man, maybe still in his twenties, wearing exquisitely fine clothes which appeared to be Muslin. Four heavy gold rings, each inlaid with a gem, flashed on his fingers. He shook the man by his shoulders, but the man was insensible to any physical stimulus. He seemed to be drugged. The bonfire was dying out.

Now, he could take no chance. He hefted the lanky frame on his shoulder and ran off into the jungle. Another roar from the depth of the jungle mercilessly cut through the veil of silence. It was closing in. Something slithered in the undergrowth nearby. But he was, by now, beyond caring about these trivialities. He knew that probably he had about half an hour or so before the dacoits woke up. Then, seeing their victim gone, all hell would break loose.

He was panting by now, and sweating profusely as he ran. He had been running in the forest for more than half an hour at least. The young man on his shoulder, despite his lanky frame, appeared to weigh one ton. He could not carry on unless he rested awhile. So, he gently put the man down on a patch of grass, nearby, with his back supported by a thick tree trunk and dropped down beside him.

Here, the trees were less dense. The canopy of the foliage overhead was broken a bit. Starlight filtered down making forms vaguely discernible. The young man sat where he was put, head lolling on his thin chest. Now it was time to break his spell of insensible slumber. There was no water was at hand which he could splash on his face. So he took recourse to the next best option. He grabbed the long hair of the man with his left hand and began slapping him hard repeatedly across his face with his right, First a moan escaped from the youngster's lips. Then he began to struggle. After that he opened his eyes, fully awake.

"Who are you?" the hapless young man asked. "Are you one of them?" His voice was a mere whisper that was barely audible.

"No, I am not." he replied. "But who are you? How come you are here in such a state?"

The young man heaved a sigh and changed his position. Then he gently massaged his wrists. The binding cords had been very tight!

"You can't get me some water, I suppose? Ah, well! My story! You see, it is a long one."

"Be brief. We don't have the whole night. The dacoits are probably awake by now."

As the young man took in a deep breath and made to begin what could be a long story, he was cut off.

"Before you begin, I'd like to ask you another question. It seems very odd to me, as if I am in the wrong place, at the wrong time. Could you please tell me what year it is and what month is?"

"Why? It is 1240, and the month is Ashwin! Or didn't you know?"

"Wait, wait. What is that by the English reckoning? Julian calendar, I mean."

The young man peered at him, utterly unfazed at the weirdness of the question. He knew the calendar the Englishmen followed, but it was very unusual for anyone, not in the payroll of the English, to opt for the English calendar, not the Bengali one.

"It is 1833 A.D. and the month is September!"

Our man emitted a low whistle. By some vagaries of fate he had flipped back 179 years in time.

"So, the British East India Company is now ruling the roost? Are they?"

"Of course they are with Lord William Bentinck as the Governor General."

"William Bentinck? Then Raja Rammohan Roy...sati..." The pages from his school history book seemed to come alive.

"Yes indeed! You have heard of the Raja?"

"Oh yes!"

"But who are you, friend? You look like us, speak like us, yet you seem to be coming from a foreign country".

"That can wait. Now tell me your story."

The young man was a zamindar who lived in the so called Black Town of Calcutta. He had his own palatial building in the Baghbazar area, overlooking the River Ganga. At this, the listener drew in a sharp breath.

The youngster had his zamindari in the Birbhum area of Bengal, but they were absentee landlords, living in Calcutta. Three to four times a year he visited his estate to settle all administrative and financial things. This time, with a few of his employees and bodyguards, he had visited his village about a fortnight ago. Three days ago he was on his way back to Calcutta, with the money collected as tax from his tenants and subjects. This jungle, about fifteen miles from Calcutta, was their last hurdle and they were in a hurry to get across this dangerous stretch in the daytime. But, as luck would have it, they were waylaid by a band of dacoits. It was total massacre. Most of the bodyguards had fled and those who could not, were killed mercilessly. The money collected was looted and the zamindar was captured alive. A message was sent to his wife and mother in Calcutta, demanding a hefty sum as ransom. If this ransom was not paid within the week, the young zamindar would be sacrificed on the altar of Kali on the next new moon night.

At this, our man stood up and stretched, stifling a yawn.

"Now we must be off or the dacoits will be coming after us."

The young zamindar stood up and caught hold of his hands in gratitude.

"All my life I shall remember what you have done for me."

"If we do not start now, 'all your life' would mean nothing much." he said, starting to walk away in long strides. The young man almost ran behind him and caught hold of his arm.

"But you didn't tell me your name or where you come from." said the young man.

"Oh, I am Hari Singh from a small village near Calcutta, called Barasat." How effortlessly all of it came out. But who was Hari Singh? Certainly not he! He was someone else! But why did it feel that he was Hari Singh? Why did the vision of a tiny hut in a quaint village flash in his mind's eye? Why did it feel that his wife and little daughter were waiting for him? "But you didn't tell me your name."

"I am called Birbikram Sen." The name struck a chord somewhere, but where?

Suddenly from afar a cry arose. It was a human cry, a blood-curdling, spine chilling wail of a doomed man together with the thunderous roar of an enraged tiger. This was immediately followed by a din of several voices yelling together. The cry, "Kill" was heard above the cacophony. The tiger roared again. The bonfire must have died out. The tiger had found its victim. Then all was still. The tiger had become the victim.

"Run." cried Birbikram and they ran like men possessed. At last they came upon a clearing in the forest. By this time they were exhausted to the point of breaking down as they stood panting. This unaccustomed exercise was killing them both. Both of them now stood with their hands on their waists and doubled over as they panted. Birbikram retched and tried to throw up, but it was an ineffectual, dry effort. It was the effect of drugs on an empty stomach, compounded by the intense struggle to stay alive.

A noise startled them. It was as if several people were spread over a wide area and were advancing steadily, calling out to keep in touch with each other. The escape of the victim had been noticed. The chase had begun. Hari pulled Birbikram's hand back to make him stop as he listened hard with all his senses attuned to catch the faintest of sounds.

"They are closing in." he whispered. "They have spread out to search wider areas. Something has to be done."

"But what can we do?" Birbikram's voice was tremulous.

"Separate. Each of us must go in a different direction. This will confuse them. We stand a better chance of escaping this way." Now they could vaguely make out each other's features. The eastern sky, unseen from where they stood, was shimmering with the the pale fingers of the first light of dawn.

"See that trail?" Hari pointed. Indeed a narrow jungle trail, probably used more by animals than man, could be discerned in the undergrowth. "Take that. Run as fast as you can. You may chance upon the main road. It should run along that way." The young man had to be saved!

Birbikram looked at Hari. He came up to him. They hugged wordlessly. Then Birbikram turned and ran along the trail without a second look back.

Hari stood there for a while, undecided as to which direction he should take. The slowly increasing light made travel through the jungle easier, but it would also make spotting easier. He turned to the opposite direction and ran.

The cries could now be heard quite close by. There was a concerted yell. He had been spotted by his hunters! He swerved in the opposite direction and ran as fast as his tired feet could carry him. Another shout! This time from his front! He was surrounded and the noose was tightening. He swerved again and ran on. He was not giving in that easily. Then he saw the stone lying in his path. Swooping low, as he ran, without breaking his step, he picked up the heavy stone with one hand the fingers closing in tightly in a throwing grip.

"Catch him alive! Don't let him go!" a voice bellowed from behind him, too close for comfort. He swivelled on the ball of his left heel with the grace of a ballet dancer; saw a hefty figure with a large moustache and a larger scowl, carrying a spear in his left hand and a huge sword in the right; bent his body back and in one fluid movement, threw the stone straight at the grimacing face. He threw with all his might as if his life depended on it, as it indeed it did. There was a mighty thud and a sickening crunch of bone breaking. A cry arose, "Sardar! He has killed the sardar! Kill the bastard!" He turned and ran again.

The figure in front of him stood still as if carved in ebony. Time was caught as if in slow motion. Slowly the man unslung the bow from his shoulder and fitted an arrow. He pulled and released it with a twang! The arrow whirred along straight towards Hari. He could see the feathers stuck to the shaft. It whirled rapidly as it cut through the air. A golden ray of the rising sun fell on the merciless arrowhead. It struck Hari on the chest, to the right of his left nipple. A searing pain ripped his chest apart. Then all went black.

He woke with a start. The dazzling light of the morning sun hurt his eyes. His shirt had dried up only to be drenched with sweat. His jeans were still damp, so were his sneakers. In his right hand he held on to the polythene packet. He was still sitting in the bus. Sheepishly he stood up. There was no one around, neither the conductor nor the driver. He alighted from the bus. It was an old run-down bus that had seen better days, parked at the side of the road, perhaps waiting for the van to come to tow it away to some junk yard. All around him the city had come to life. He took his prescription out from the wrappings. It had his name printed clearly on the top. "Mr. Sandip Sen" it read. Yes, that was his name. His age too, was recorded. Forty two, it said. He now felt a burning sensation in his chest. Will the excruciating pain return? But it did not. There was only a burning sensation. He hailed a passing taxi and climbed in, telling the driver his home address. "Baghbazar," he said, "near the Ganga".

As he settled in the taxi, he unbuttoned his shirt to look at his birthmark. It was angry red in appearance. Birbikram! Suddenly the name came back to him. He had heard the name from his grandmother. In his old books he had come across a diary. On the first page, was a beautifully calligraphed signature, 'Birbikram Sen'. He was one of his illustrious forefathers. His grandmother had said. She had died three years ago, his last remaining relative. The sprawling mansion was kept under lock and key as he only used a couple of rooms and one bathroom. The rest of the mansion – or should he say, palace? – were occasionally rented out to film groups for shooting. This at least provided the money for maintenance.

Reaching home, Sandip went straight to the cupboard and took out Birbikram's diary. He leafed through the pages till he came upon the entry he was looking for. It read:

10th Ashwin, 1240: Had a narrow escape from the hands of dacoits. A man, Hari Singh, from Barasat village, saved my life. Where is he now? How is he? I hope he could escape. I am here today, just because he had risked his own life that I may live.

On the...

Sandip put the diary down, immersed in thought. He kept it back to where it belonged. As he undressed for a bath, he noticed the birthmark again. It glistened red.

He never had that pain again.

✦ ✦ ✦

10

The Lonely Young Man

I met him almost every other day. He was a lanky young man, standing there, alone, in his favourite posture of a leaning tower of Pisa, propped up by the kindly lamp-post set in the corner of the street. Sometimes I wondered what this guy would have done had the municipality not been thoughtful enough to provide him with this prop! But the municipality is humane, so this eventuality never came to be.

The street made an abrupt right angled turn exactly at this spot. So the lamp-post was very strategically located. It was one of the three main roads on the way to and from the local market place and, therefore, very busy in the morning hours when the townspeople rushed there for their daily provisions, coming back exhausted and more often than not, exasperated at the high prices of eatables. The afternoons, especially in the hot summer months, were generally quiet, with a few stragglers wandering about and even fewer stray dogs looking for a bit of shade. Close by, stood the ramshackle tea stall, run by the never-say-die optimist, Bhulo, who knew it all, from Sachin Tendulkar to Baba Amte. His tea stall as well as the barber shop run by Babu, just up the street, were two bulletin boards in the neighbourhood. One did not need any newspaper or news channel to keep abreast with all that was happening in the country and abroad, if one cared to patronize these two places. But Bhulo's stall stole a march over Babu's in that it was a hotbed of local gossip. Therefore, it was strange that Bhulo had nothing to do with this lanky leaning tower. In fact, it seemed as if Bhulo and he avoided contact. Perhaps he was a long standing debtor of Bhulo and his credit was written off as a bad debt, or perhaps this man, I did not know his name, suffered from an unnamed tropical inflammation of the liver and abstained from tea. Whatever it was, they were not even in eye contact relation and that I found strange, given that both frequented the same street corner.

This part of the town was relatively sparsely populated, and that I found to be a strange paradox. The real estate people preferred to stay away from this area. But in the rest of the town people lived cheek to jowl. Several ownership flats were coming up with the promoters, as it was said, literally minting money everywhere. But this area had strangely been overlooked by them.

"No dada, it's not that." said Netai, a contractor by profession, as he blew into his tumbler of morning tea at Bhulo's shop.

"Then what could be the reason?" I asked.

Netai set his tea down and eyed Bhulo through the corner of his slightly squinted eye. Bhulo was busy stirring a spoonful of sugar in a fresh tumbler.

"That building you see there." said Netai, pointing towards a broken down edifice across the street. "That house has a bad reputation. That's why people generally stay away from this place."

"Why?" I asked. "What's wrong with it?"

"Ah, well, ahem...actually that house has the dubious distinction of being haunted."

"A haunted house!" I exclaimed, looking at the building with renewed interest.

The house in question could hardly be called a house any longer. It was more of a heap of rubble. The roof appeared to have caved in. One of the four pillars of the portcullis was gone. The window shutters were all broken leaving yawning gaps in the rundown walls, or at least of the parts of the walls that were still standing. The grounds were overgrown with weeds. No wonder people gave this place a wide berth. It was the house of the local zamindar, a Roy Bahadur to boot. But with the abolition of the zamindari system, this house had fallen into disuse. The last of the owners resided in Kolkata, where they had a flourishing business manufacturing underwear. There they had their own palatial establishment, cars and what not! They had even sent their children abroad to get 'foreign education'. They had no reason to cling to their past. Unfortunately this edifice, here, was riddled by court cases in the matter of ownership and succession amongst the last of the lawful owners, so that it could not be sold off. But who would take it? At nights, especially on full moon nights, this building appeared to come alive, with footfalls and laughter echoing through the dilapidated corridors.

All this information was supplied to me by the tea-stall owner, Bhulo. As I had said earlier, he was a master of local folklore. I was relatively new to this place, having come to stay here only a few months ago. In the course of my Government service I had been posted in different towns all over the state of West Bengal, and had come here but recently. This town had, somehow, been connected to me in a distant past, through the aegis of my great-uncle, Darpanarayan Banerjee. His faded sepia portrait used to hang from a wall in my ancestral home. The photograph was somewhat hazy too, or smudgy. I do not know whether this was because of the poor quality of photography in those days, or whether time had taken its toll. He, from what I had heard, had been a great scholar and spent a lifetime in the service of Bishwambhar Roy, the local zamindar. He had worked faithfully under the choleric zamindar of a tyrannical disposition, till he died of consumption when he was just thirty-six years of age. I knew that this rundown house had been the ancestral home of Bishwambhar, but I did not know all the details, till I had met the local chronicler, Bhulo.

"But, Bhulo, aren't you afraid of running your tea-stall here?" I asked.

"Why should I be?" asked Bhulo in wonder. "I run my business in the morning hours, don't I? I cater to Babus like you, who are coming back from market. By the afternoon I am generally off to mind the other stall of mine in the town, which is looked after by my wife during the morning hours. And everybody knows that 'they' never disturb anyone during daytime."

I admired his hard core logic.

The young man was still there at his post. I could only say this much about him that he was a great minder of his own business. He kept himself to himself. He simply stood there watching life go by, never talking to anyone, nor raising his hand to greet anyone. Not that he was discourteous, though. He smiled always, whenever I caught his eyes, and I smiled back.

That day I could not resist myself. After the formalities of brief exchange of smiles were taken care of, I walked over to where he stood, or rather leaned.

"Good morning." I said. The young man straightened. He was quite tall and fair, though slightly built with a mass of unkempt hair partly obscuring his charming visage. He was in his early thirties, I guessed.

"Good morning." he greeted me in return, with a smile that lit up his countenance.

"You don't mind me talking to you, do you?" I asked.

"Why should I?" The young man was bewildered.

"No, but I think that I am disturbing you."

"You are doing nothing of that sort. You see, it feels good to talk to someone after such a long time. No one talks to me these days, I suppose you have noticed it." he added.

"I see you standing here every day. I was just curious to know why." I said.

"I love watching people scurrying about in their daily routine."

"But why do you keep standing here every day? Are you looking for someone?"

"You could say that, I suppose."

"But what do you do for a living?" I asked, somehow knowing perfectly well at the back of my mind that I would not get a clear answer.

"Living is it? Well, I write." came the brief and simple reply.

"Oh, you are a writer?" I asked foolishly.

"Sort of you can say. Right now I am working on the history of this place."

"Then you are a scholar." I said, relieved at having reached a definite conclusion.

"Yes, that I am."

"History means the locale, the people, the zamindars..."

"Right you are."

"But, still, you are an enigma to me. I often wonder who you are, where you are from, and questions like these keep forming in my mind."

"I could tell you all, but my friend, it may take some time." He said giving me a cool appraisal from head to foot. I glanced at the leafy vegetables and the tail-end of the Rohu fish peeping over the top of the market bag I held in my right hand. What the hell, thought I. The wife was away in Kolkata and I was alone at home. The lady who came in to cook my meals was not due for at least a couple of hours now and today was a Sunday.

"I have time. Lots, in fact." I said with a smile. He nodded and led me to an ancient wooden bench set under a tamarind tree and sat down, inviting me to do the same.

"Look, I am not a very good conversationist, but I don't know why, ever since I saw you first I felt that I know you."

"That's nice." I said, as I took my seat. "Now tell me about yourself." The young man was silent for a long, long time.

"Do you really want to know?" he asked.

"Oh yes, I do." I replied even as I steeled myself to hear woeful tales of frustration and possible recounts of a murky past. But what he told me was totally unexpected.

The young man drew a deep breath, and squared his shoulders. His eyes were focussed straight as if at an infinite point. Then he uttered in a sepulchral voice, "I am a ghost!"

"Ok, that's nice...What! A ghost!" I almost jumped out of my skin.

"Yes, of the horror story kind." With this profoundly revealing statement he looked at my face and stared intently to see whether my expression changed or not.

"Ah, come on my friend." I said, sitting back again on the ancient bench after I got my breath back. "That can hardly be possible. You can't be a ghost."

"Why not?" he challenged me.

"Ghosts, if at all they exist, can be seen only at night. But this is broad daylight, man!" I exclaimed.

"So that's the way you think, do you?" the young man said. "Now, let me give you a sensible lecture. How many hours are there in a day?" Seeing that I was silent at this dumb sort of a question, he carried on. "Twenty-four, isn't it? Approximately half of it is day and half is night. It concludes that if a ghost has to exist, he has to stick around at some place in the daytime as well. Isn't it so?"

At this, I became very thoughtful and scratched my chin. This ghost, if he was a ghost at all, was a logical one.

"Ok, since you insist, Mr. Ghost...but you must be living somewhere..."

"There you touch a nerve. Yes, indeed I live somewhere. I live in the run down palace that you can see there. But it will no longer be my home for long. You see, there are quite a handful of us who have taken up abode at this place. But soon some promoter will grab the property and a brand new structure with mortar, bricks, glass and aluminium will come up, with dazzling lights and countless people romping about...well, where does that leave us? We'll be rendered homeless in no time. This has been the story of all urban ghosts, but the same thing will start here as well. Oh, I am so sad!" He sniffed. Just imagine! One snivelling ghost!

"This is serious matter. So what will you do now?"

"I am not sure. I have really grown to love this place, you know." the ghost said almost to himself. "That is also my reason for standing here at a stretch every day. I want to capture the place in my mind's eye." I hemmed and cleared my throat preparing for the next question.

"Have you been around here for long?"

"Not really. I think it has been a hundred years or so."

"Righto." said I. "But do you have to stick around here till Doomsday?"

"Of course not." came the indignant reply. "We can go onwards, although I have failed to do so till now."

"But why?" I asked.

"There are fixed prerequisites for that. I mean you have to fulfil certain obligations before you are allowed to go on. Two things need to be done, but I have failed on both counts."

"What are they?" I could hardly contain my curiosity.

"One is doing someone a really good turn. The other is scaring someone out of his wits. I could do neither. You see, I had never been a very enterprising type."

"Then that is a real problem." I said.

"There is another provision also. If I am recognized and remembered by someone of my own blood I may be allowed to move on. But that too has proved a near impossibility so far as I don't really belong to this area."

"Well, best of luck in you quest." I said, standing up. It was getting late. There are better ways of spending a Sunday morning than chatting with a non-enterprising ghost.

The ghost stood up too. He hugged his lanky frame with both his arms as if suffering from a sudden attack of ague.

"So are you going away too?" he asked.

"I have to now." I said. "It is already late. By the way, you didn't tell me your name."

"There is no need to. You know me well enough." he said looking into my eyes. A chill ran down my spine suddenly. Yes, I have seen those eyes before. But where? I could not be sure. They seemed so familiar, yet unfamiliar. I was utterly confused.

"Don't look at me like that." I said, visibly disturbed. "You remind me of someone."

"I do? Who do I remind you of?" A touch of sarcastic smile touched the angle of his mouth. Then it came to me. In fact the realization hit me like an express train and my hair stood on end.

"My great-uncle, Darpanarayan Banerjee, long deceased."

"Took a long time, didn't you?" Then he started laughing. It was blood chilling laughter. It came in waves swirling around me, to engulf me. I dropped my bag and shut my ears to cut it off. But the laughter seemed to go round and round in my head, reverberating within my skull. His image began to shimmer strangely. Then it started breaking up into small fragments to be blown away by a sudden gust of cold wind.

Far away in a village home the thread of a sepia photograph hanging from a wall, broke loose and the photo crashed down to the floor, the glass shattering into a thousand pieces.

✦ ✦ ✦

11

A Punctured Tyre

Sujit was in a great hurry. The sun had set and dusk was closing in, too rapidly for comfort. He had aimed at crossing the awe inspiring open fields of the infamous Thyangarer Maath while there was still daylight. But now it appeared that he would not be able to do so. His ancient scooter was already being pushed to its limits. The old faithful was spluttering along with all its might, as if, it too, was aware of the intentions of its owner. Suddenly there was a fierce "hiss". The scooter wobbled and almost ran out of control. Sujit pressed on the brake pedal hard. There was a screech and the scooter almost keeled over. Nevertheless it came to a stop. Sujit alighted and so did Anwar, his assistant, who was riding the pillion. The rear tyre had gone flat. Sujit put the scooter up on its stand and wiped his face with a grimy handkerchief. Not a soul was in sight. The landscape all around, was drab and featureless dotted about with clumps of stunted trees and occasional paddy fields. The road snaked through this open expanse like a languid black python. The wind rose as Anwar put in the wheels-jack, preparing for a change of tyre, muttering under his breath the old Bengali proverb, *"Jekhanei Baagher bhoy, sekhanei sondhye hoy!"* (Where there is the danger of a tiger, the dusk settles in).

Sujit was a young medic, a physician to be precise, attached to the Government hospital in a small subdivisional town in West Bengal, about 150 km from Kolkata. As a town it had nothing much to speak about, but the 300-bed hospital was very well equipped and staffed by young enthusiastic doctors. Consequently it was always overcrowded and the doctors overworked. Sujit's ancestral village was in these parts. Therefore, in spite of his hectic schedule he was happy out here as he could identify himself with the locale.

Sujit's daily schedule did not leave much breathing space for him. His relatively easier day was Sunday. Therefore, when he chose this day to go away for his rural practice his wife had been a bit crestfallen. But these rural visits were needed to build up his practice. So she had given in, with a bit of reluctance, Thus every Sunday after breakfast, Sujit wheeled his old scooter out and, accompanied by his compounder Anwar, scooted over the eighty odd kilometres, visiting his clinics in three different villages set well apart.

Sujit loved this weekly sojourn. These visits gave him the opportunity to see the real face of rural Bengal. He loved the small hamlets set in groves of trees of different sorts, the sparkling ponds with a greenish tinge, the waddling ducks marching in columns as solemnly as if on a funeral march, the paddy fields. Everything. He loved his old scooter and loved riding bare-headed as the wind played through his hair and over his face. It was his escape from the rigours of the daily humdrum known as life.

Thyangarer Maath – the name itself sent a chill down the spine. The first village outside the town limits was Sitan. Beyond this village there was an immense expanse of apparently no-man's land, before one came upon the next village, Madanpur, some seven or eight kilometres away. The fields, for the most parts were arid and fallow, with a few areas of arable land. This was the infamous Thyangarer Maath. Thyangare was the name given to a specific brand of highwaymen who made life miserable for travellers in the days of the East India Company's rule in Bengal. They used to hide beside the highway with two sticks. The shorter stick, also known as *phabra,* was thrown at a lightning speed at the feet of the lone traveller. It invariably brought him down, often with legs broken. Then he was set upon by the dacoits, who often murdered for pennies. Lord William Bentinck, the Governor General, brought all this to a stop. Possibly the open fields had been the haunts of *Thyangares* in the distant past. The Thyangares have gone, but the name had stuck. The fields, however, lived up to their evil repute. In these days dacoits still waited out there to pounce upon unsuspecting travellers and robbed them of all their belongings. Police patrol vehicles made their routine rounds of the area, but to little avail. On his way back from his rural clinics Sujit had to cross these fields, every Sunday evening, to reach his residence.

It was all Nakur Kaka's fault. He had absolutely no business coming over to his Kirtihat clinic, but he had and had sat chatting with him, thereby eating mercilessly Sujit's time. But Sujit could hardly refuse him. Nakur Kaka was from his own village and a distant relative as well. Now he was settled in Kirtihat, a local business centre, looking after his flourishing business in aluminium products. Once he had very close family ties with Sujit's family. He had come in when Sujit was attending to his patients. Not content with exchanging pleasantries, he had insisted that Sujit accompany him to his home for a cup of tea after he had done with seeing patients. Sujit could not refuse his offer.

Actually it was Anwar who was more tense about crossing the Thyangarer Maath after dark. Sujit was more secure in his 'left-right indicator' schedule. A few days ago, Akash had come to his clinic. He was a young man with a pleasant disposition who used to work at a chemist's shop outside the hospital. He came from the village of Madanpur and was very resourceful. He addressed Sujit as 'dada' or elder brother.

Akash had come to his clinic just as he was about to leave. He knocked as he entered.

"Dada, I have something to tell you."

"Yes?" asked Sujit.

"Every Sunday you come alone across Thyangarer Maath, in the evening. This is a bit risky, you know." said Akash. "I am a local man and tell you that the fields are not a very safe place to travel through after dark."

"I know, Akash. But I never travel alone. Anwar is always with me."

"Whatever..." Akash was quiet for a while. His demeanour said that he had something more to add.

"You see, dada, I come from Madanpur and I have to cross the field every day. One has many friends in that area, especially if one is born and brought up there, you know. I bring you a message from those who are your well wishers."

"What is it?" Sujit's curiosity knew no bounds.

"If it becomes dark on your way back, you are to light your indicators, first left, then right, and continue like this for about five seconds cycles, alternately, till you are through across the fields. The people concerned will recognize that it is you who is crossing and there will be no mishap whatsoever."

On his way back that day, Sujit was religiously applying this 'left-right indicator' principle, but he wanted to cross the area at the earliest, nevertheless, for one never knew what could happen in a case of mistaken identity.

As Anwar proceeded to change the tyre, replacing the punctured one with the spare one Sujit lit a cigarette and looked around. He was tense and rightly so. Light was fading rapidly as the orange of the western sky was being replaced by a more purplish hue. The wide expanse of the flat, arid landscape all around was slowly darkening, as all features were being smudged by the incoming tide of darkness. Incongruously the old fairy tale, heard so many years ago, came back to Sujit's mind, that demons became most powerful at this time of the day.

"Got a light, dada?"

The sudden, sepulchral voice made Sujit almost jump out of his skin. A tall, lanky, middle aged man, with a three-day growth of salt and pepper beard and bushy moustache to match, was standing beside him. Sujit had not seen him coming. Where did he spring from, he wondered. The guy was dressed in a white, once clean shirt and khaki trousers. He carried an ordinary gunny bag in his right hand and had an unlighted bidi hanging from his lips.

"Have you got a light on you?" the man repeated his question in a roundabout way. Sujit silently gave him his lighter. The man lit up and drew deeply on his bidi, before he handed the lighter back to Sujit.

"You folks are in a fix, I see. Can I lend a hand?"

"No need. Thanks all the same." Anwar tersely replied on Sujit's behalf.

"Don't take it otherwise. I just offered to help because this place does not have a good reputation, especially this second bend of the S-shaped curve." He drew on his bidi with a vengeance.

Sujit looked about him. True enough. They were indeed standing at the second bend of the road, where the road became S-shaped.

"Why? What's so special about this place?" asked Sujit.

The man came up closer to whisper in his ear. A whiff of stale sweat, rancid breath and cheap tobacco filled Sujit's nostril.

"Murder, dear sir. Murders have taken place here."

"Is that so?" In spite of his bravado Sujit's limbs had gone cold.

"Sir, it is ready now." Anwar called out. Sujit nodded with relief and walked up to his scooter.

"But who are you, sir?" Sujit called out to the stranger. "Aren't you afraid of this place? You are alone I can see."

"I am Sri Nabakumar Sarkhel of Madanpur. No sir. Nothing will happen to me. I am not afraid. Not any more."

The tone of his voice felt strange in Sujit's ears. However, he did not pay any heed and mounting his scooter he kicked it to life. Anwar climbed up behind him. Sujit switched the headlights on, although some of the fading daylight still remained. He turned back to bid the stranger good bye, but peculiarly enough, the man was nowhere to be seen! It was as if he had emerged from the ensuing darkness and had disappeared into it.

Akash came to meet him the very next morning.

"Heard that you were stranded in the Thyangarer Maath last evening?" asked Akash.

"Who told you? No one saw us there!" Sujit was incredulous. Akash smiled.

"We have our sources."

"But who could it be? Oh, of course! Nabakumar Sarkhel of Madanpur. He must have told you."

Akash almost fell out of his chair.

"Who, sir? Who did you say?"

"Nabakumar Sarkhel! A thin built man with a three day old stubble! Why? You ought to know him. He is from Madanpur, he said. That's your own village, isn't it?"

"Are you sure, dada?"

"Of course I am súre."

"But Nabakumar Sarkhel is dead, sir. He was murdered on the road running through Thyangarer Maath, right where it makes an 'S' curve."

"What do you mean?" Sujit was astounded.

"Nabakumar was a cattle merchant. He was returning from the market, one Sunday evening, about six years ago. He was murdered for cash. That was the last murder in that area."

That afternoon saw Sujit at the Railway Station, waiting to board the Kolkata bound train. He was going to book a car.

The story has been previously published online in 'Your Story Club' in June 2012.

✦ ✦ ✦

12

They Drink at Night

The silence was eerie. A regular chirping of crickets had a near hypnotic effect on the surroundings. The landscape was flooded with the quicksilver light of the full moon. All shadows were accentuated in such a way that could only be seen swathed in moonlight. A silvery streak gleamed a short distance away, denoting the mountain stream that flowed out there. This was where the animals came down to drink. The land, devoid of vegetation in this stretch, gently sloped downhill towards the stream, across which it swooped up again to form the rows of rolling hills, rising step by step, as if in tiers. It was that sort of a night when all senses got heightened to a preternatural level. An occasional rustling in the undergrowth heralded the passage of some unseen animal, most probably a predator, accounting for the spooky silence that prevailed. Big cats were rare in this area. But, of course, this was leopard country. Abhijit reached for his glass of vodka and tonic kept on the table to his left and, at the same time, wrapped the shawl closer round his broad shoulders. The nights were chilly.

Virendra came up with a lantern emanating more soot than light. Electricity had made some inroads in some parts of this wilderness but the forest and this bungalow had been bypassed till now, due to some obvious reasons. A slow, ponderous beat of drums from afar broke through the reverie of silence. The tribal workers of some far away tea garden were enjoying themselves after an arduous day of hard work. Abhijit waved Virendra's ineffectual lantern away. He preferred the darkness, the moonlight, his vodka and his solitude. Light encroached upon his privacy.

With the help of the dim light Virendra scanned the table for the supply of provisions and then limped away, the floorboards creaking under his feet. Virendra Singh Thapa was the caretaker of this forest bungalow. He was an interesting old-timer on superannuation, and was possibly as old as Methuselah.

On his way back Virendra stopped suddenly, peered about in a short sighted manner, and came back to Abhijit.

"Sir," he mumbled in Nepali, a language Abhijit was perfectly at home with, having served as the District Forest Officer for quite some time in these parts. "Sir, please be on your alert. The big cats are out."

"I know, Virendra *daju*, and I am alert. Now, please take the lantern away. The light is hurting my eyes. And get me some more fried chicken, will you? There's a good man." Abhijit's eyes roved towards the loaded gun hanging from a nail in the wall. He was a good shot with a better night sight than many. But he preferred to shoot with his handycam rather than a gun.

The gun was there mainly to boost his own confidence and scare off intruders if the need arose.

The offending light was removed forthwith and Abhijit took a thoughtful sip of vodka. Now he had heaps of time on his hand. All his life he had roamed about in forests in different parts of West Bengal till his retirement at the end of a long and lusterless tenure in this part of the Dooars region. He had no family to speak of. Never had any. He had been a self-sufficient confirmed bachelor all through his life. There was no earthly reason for his remaining a bachelor, only that there had never been an occasion to shed his 'bachelor' degree. At the back of his mind, he knew, though, that is was a fitting tribute to someone he had been in love with, a thousand years ago. He smiled to himself and shifted in his seat. Then, suddenly, he froze. The gleaming streak of the stream was no longer visible from where he sat, being obscured by a mass of moving black shadows. A faint gurgling and splashing could be heard. Elephants, he thought. They have come down for a drink.

A barely audible creaking announced Virendra's arrival with a plate heaped with fried chickens. Midway across the veranda he stopped in his tracks and peered about.

"Elephants, sir," he whispered, barely audible. "Coming down for a drink. This group always drinks at night."

"Yes, I've seen them." said Abhijit in a barely audible murmur, for he knew that a whisper carries a much greater distance than a toned down murmur. He just hoped, nay, prayed that Samir did not come barging in at this point of time. He glanced at the luminous dial of his wristwatch. It was barely seven, yet in the forest it seemed to be the dead of night.

Samir was a childhood friend of Abhijit. Both were approximately the same age and had been to the same school. They were both ardent sportsmen and played soccer and cricket together in the same local club. Abhijit was a good cricketer and had gone on to play for his school, college and then for the university. Samir's prowess was more to be seen on the football field and he was the club captain at one time. They had been so very inseparable that their friends called them 'twins'. Some of them had further qualified this, adding the prefix 'Siamese' to the 'twins'. Their path had separated only when they entered college. After that, they graduated and Abhijit had joined the Forest Service, while Samir started his own dealership of electronic goods. Samir had married fairly early in life. The couple had remained childless for about five years or so, after which their only son was born. This boy was now in Germany studying for a degree in Engineering. Recently, Samir had lost his wife.

It was Abhijit who had made the programme. He had gone to visit some relatives in Kolkata and there he had met his friend after a long gap. The reunion was a happy one, though Samir was still depressed at the loss of his wife. Abhijit had suggested that he would make arrangements for the two of them to spend a quiet weekend at this forest bungalow. Samir had readily agreed to the proposal.

Samir was on his way back from town, where he had gone to buy provisions. After a long time he was feeling really relaxed. The forest had its own charm and attracted him in such a way that he had never thought would be possible. All his life he had been a diehard Kolkatan, or rather Calcatian, as lifelong residents of this great metropolis preferred to call themselves. He had seldom travelled far, and the little he had travelled was all for business, within India and abroad. After coming to this place at the insistence of Abhijit, he had felt his tension gradually ebbing away. The hollow feeling following the death of his wife was no longer there, although the ache remained. He was grateful to Abhijit for planning this vacation and longed to do something worthwhile in return. Therefore, when the question of getting provisions from the local market came up, Samir had grabbed the opportunity with both hands.

It had been broad daylight when Samir had set forth on his quest in the Forest Department jeep with only the driver Madan Singh to keep him company. The two were a study in contrast. While Madan Singh was a burly man, quite tall, with a bushy moustache, Samir was thin built, clean shaven and totally suave and urbane in all respects. Yet they struck an immediate rapport and Madan Singh pointed out to him all the exotic flora and fauna they came across on their way. In the town Samir spent very little time shopping and soon they were on their way back with bags of grocery, chicken and other essential items like a few bottles of life saving beverage. On the way back Samir opened a bottle and sampled some of the liquor he had procured, finding it to be absolutely to his satisfaction. The spirit soon lifted Samir's mood and he began humming the tune of a Hindi film song that had been in vogue in their student days. All was going well till they turned into the road that led straight through the forest. Madan Singh applied the brakes hard and turned off the ignition.

"Madan, what's wrong?" asked Samir in consternation. Madan put his index finger on his lips making the international sign of total silence. Then he leaned over to whisper in Samir's ears.

"Elephants, sahib."

"How do you know?" Samir asked incredulously.

Madan silently pointed to a heap of droppings plumb in the centre of the road. Even Samir's city bred eyes could make out that the droppings were fairly recent. He looked at Madan Singh questioningly. Silently Madan Singh gestured to him to stay put and reached into the back seat to fetch the big gun he had brought with him. He put up his hand to assure Samir that all was well and this was just a precaution. They then settled down to wait.

Abhijit was really worried now. Samir should have been back at least by sunset. He got up from his armchair and began pacing the veranda. This was a long time habit of his. But he had to desist soon as the floor boards creaked. Suddenly Virendra clutched at the hem of Abhijit's kurta.

"Sir," whispered he. "They leave now."

Sure enough, the great black shadows were moving away. Abhijit heaved a sigh of relief.

Within a short time the muffled roar of a jeep's engine was heard as the vehicle turned and crunched up the moonlit gravel pathway of the bungalow with headlights switched off. Virendra hurried down to retrieve all the provisions that he knew to be loaded in the jeep. Samir stumbled in the dark as he clambered up the wooden stairs to the veranda.

"What took you so long?" said Abhijit. "I've been worrying my head off!"

"Mahakal! We stopped to pay homage to the overlord of the jungle."

"You are drunk." complained Abhijit.

"Huh! No more than you are pal." quipped Samir. "But I wouldn't call it a drink. Ugh! In Styrofoam cups too!" Abhijit smiled. The forest was gradually bringing the old Samir out.

Samir sat down on the vacant armchair on the other side of the low coffee-table. He picked up Abhijit's empty glass and sniffed.

"What are you having? Ah! Vodka with tonic! Downright civilized, aren't you?" He called for Virendra and instructed him to bring water, slices of lemon, green chilies and salt.

"Now I'll show you how vodka should be drunk. But, hey! Can't we have some music? Something soothing, from the sixties or seventies?"

"Are you mad?" Abhijit exclaimed. "You are in the jungle, pal, in the midst of wild animals! Or have you forgotten? Just sit still and enjoy the music of the moonlit forest."

The clock in the hall downstairs gently chimed ten. The distant drum-beats had ceased for quite some time now. The two cronies were by now deep into the reminiscence of their youthful days.

"It was hilarious, wasn't it?" Samir said. "I can still see it in my mind. There you were, stranded near the tramline close to the Shyambazar Tram Depot, with your slippers stuck to the molten asphalt and the tram clanging on for dear life right behind you! Oh God!" Samir started laughing his head off and Abhijit joined him.

"And the time when you vaulted over the railing in the Maidan to escape the mounted police's baton to land in the wide drain…" Abhijit was rolling with laughter now.

"Ah! Football! I really miss the game." Samir said.

"Yes. It was your first love. I still remember the two goals you scored in a span of three minutes against Mitali Sangha to give us the trophy."

"Yes, felt great! But you are wrong. It was not my first love, but my second."

"How come?" asked Abhijit.

"My first love was your sister, Ronjabati." declared Samir with a twinkle in his elderly eyes.

"Oh! I know that! The way you put up flashy gallery show in the football field with an eye towards our veranda spoke volumes for your emotions."

"Where is she now, Ronja?"

"They are settled in Shillong."

They sat in comfortable silence for a while, immersed in thought, sipping their own respective drunks. It was quiet all around. Only the crickets did not appear to have any sense of bedtime.

"How's Arun doing?" Abhijit broke the silence. Arun was Samir's son.

"Oh, he's doing fine. He's in Dusseldorf now. Going steady with a German girl, Stefi."

"Is it ok for you, a German daughter-in-law?"

"Of course it is. He'll probably settle there anyway. But I have no problem." said Samir while pouring a fresh drink. "He came over when his mother died. Had to go back in three days time. Very busy, young people these days. Couldn't stay for the Shradh ceremony." Samir's voice was somewhat tremulous. Or was it Abhijit's overwrought imagination?

"Now, enough of it!" Samir sat up straight. His words had started slurring a bit. In comparison Abhijit was sober. But he could hold his drink better than many. So it did not mean that he had drunk any less.

"You, my friend, had never married. Why?"

Another shadow appeared apparently floated up to the stream. Grunts and splashes followed. Bisons. It was unusual to find them moving around so late. But, perhaps this group had also made it a habit of drinking at night. Streaks of fire danced on the far away hills. Bushes were being burnt to remove weeds and make the soil more fertile than it was. Wordlessly Abhijit stood up and moved over to the balustrade. The fires danced gold in the moonlight of liquid silver. The bisons moved away.

"Hey, man, why don't you say something? You were the most eligible bachelor amongst us. From what we saw many girls swooned over you. Even then you never married. Why?"

A pair of fireflies sparkled in the bushes beyond the bungalow gates. A silent shadow slunk away. Leopard? Abhijit became alert instantly.

"Can you hear me, you oaf? Why didn't you marry?" Samir was insistent and drunk. Abhijit turned to face him.

"Because I loved your wife."

A night bird screeched and fluttered away shattering the fragile silence of the moonlit night to smithereens.

The story has been previously published online in 'Your Story Club' in July 2012.

+ + +

13

Stranded

Shyambabu was a superb driver. No other driver in any of the Governmental departments could compare with him in terms of expertise, reflexes and daring. His only problem was that he knew this thing and always strove to live up to expectation and beyond. The Medical Officer at the Sukna Health Centre, a young, enterprising doctor, called Niraj, looked to his left, then to his right and only after he was sure that there was nobody within earshot, confided in a conspiratorial tone to Satrajit.

"Sometimes he feels that he is not a driver of a Government jeep, but a helicopter pilot! So, better be alert, dada. Don't allow him a free hand with his gas pedal!"

Now, that was something to be mulled over. Shyambabu drove the Health Department jeep at Sukna. For his next Laparoscopic Sterilization camp at Ranglitar, deep into the remotest part of the Darjeeling Hills, Shyambabu was going to take the surgical team, with Satrajit as the Team Leader, in his jeep. Satrajit was a gynaecologist, posted at present at the Kurseong Subdivisional Hospital.

The morning had dawned bright and clear. This made Satrajit very happy. He would now be able to enjoy the glories of the hills to the full. The door bell rang.

"Good morning, Shyambabu. All set?"

"All set, sir."

"No fog, eh?"

"No fog, sir. The day is clear." Shyambabu knew that Satrajit did not like fog when he went for camps. Fog often rendered the visibility near zero, and this added to the hazards of journey in the hills.

Their quarters were perched up on the hillside, about 100 feet above the main hospital buildings. Fragrance of wild flowers soothed the senses as Satrajit came out of his quarter. He stopped for a while at the top of the steps to enjoy the environs.

No view could be more idyllic. The sleepy little town stretched below where he stood. The houses looked small, with some of the tin roofs reflecting the golden rays of the morning sun. Verdant hills rolled all around as far as eye could reach. The glass windows of a tea-garden factory building on the far hills, sparkled gold. To the left was the majestic snow-capped Kanchenjangha, presenting a picture postcard view under the canopy of a clear blue sky. There was a nip in the air, but this added to the overall charm of the surroundings. Birds chirped all around; bees buzzed and Satrajit felt that it was good to be alive.

The first part of the journey was straight downhill. The Pankhabari Road wound down. Soon they were past the Makaibari Tea Estate, with its green, eco friendly environs. A wide stretch of forest had been left untouched, with no human encroachment being allowed by the garden authorities since times immemorial, and Satrajit admired this. A few billboards dotted the sides of the road, cautioning the drivers not to use their horns. In one place a billboard read that vehicles were to be driven at a real slow pace, as leopards may be crossing. This was leopard zone. But the leopards here must be either very much traffic conscious or shy, most probably the latter, because Satrajit, in his numerous journeys in this area, over a number of years, was yet to encounter any spotted cat.

Near the foothills, beyond the areas dominated by tea gardens, the road levelled out, the first to cross a forest tract, reputed to be the home of elephants, then through paddy fields. Satrajit remembered that fateful evening when a tyre had given way in this haunt of elephants, after sundown, when he had to wait here for a full half hour before it had been changed and a brake problem fixed. Abject terror of pachyderms had made him shiver every single second of his waiting spell. But that was the tale of another journey, made on another day. Presently, soon enough they bypassed the bustling town of Siliguri, turning north once again, along the Sevoke Road. This time the road ran through the famous Mahananda Reserve Forest. By and by the forests were left behind and the dancing and frolicking River Teesta joined them on their right. The sun had risen well up in the sky when they turned back into the hilly stretch from Kalijhora.

They had not gone too far beyond the Latpanchor area, famous for its Cinchona and other Medicinal Plants Research Centre, when an ear-splitting 'clang' jerked Satrajit out of his reverie.

"Shyambabu, what happened?" asked Satrajit.

"Nothing to worry, Sir," said Shyambabu with a wide grin. Nothing seemed to worry this redoubtable man at all. "It is only a spring 'pati' coming loose." Parts of the spring dropping off tantamount to 'nothing' in the lexicon of this formidable man! Satrajit thought that it would be wonderful to be able to reach back home in one piece, from this endeavour.

Shyambabu was true to his word. He stopped the jeep, ran back to retrieve the offending strip of metal and dived under the vehicle to fix it by means of rubber strips, that he had conjured up from somewhere. Satrajit would not have been surprised if he saw Shyambabu using a pot of glue! He glanced towards the backseat. The members of the Nursing Staff were apparently unconcerned and were chatting away about the problems of getting their children admitted in a good school, while the anaesthetist, Akshay was rolling out a cigarette with an ashen face. His hands were trembling. Satrajit reassured him with a smile, showing a confidence that he himself scarcely felt. In the last bucket seat at the back, the OT attendant, Prem, picked his nose with such concentration as if the well being of the world depended upon his executing this task to perfection.

However, their ordeal soon came to an end, as they reached Ranglitar. A large number of patients, each sporting a tiny sticker on her forehead with her serial number, met their eyes as they alighted from their vehicle. Now they felt like ducks at the edge of a pond. They were in their element and all tension disappeared in a trice like snowflakes in April. Satrajit glanced back. Shyambabu had already dived underneath the vehicle tinkering with his chariot. Satrajit went over to crouch beside the supine man.

"Is everything ok, Shyambabu," he asked.

"Why do you worry so much, Sir? Everything is just fine!"

Why worry indeed! Satrajit had the responsibility of all his team members on his broad shoulders!

The operations began and ended by evening. In between they had partaken a hurried lunch, an exquisitely palatable local fare that the local staff members had cooked up on the open flames of pine wood.

Now, they were ready to leave. The sun had set and dusk was settling in. The second vehicle belonging to the health centre, driven by the burly Kishen Daju, was starting off to ferry the last of the patients home. He met the eyes of Satrajit and gave him a broad smile. He had known Satrajit for a number of years and held him in great respect. This feeling was mutual. Kishen's vehicle started with a roar, belching obnoxious black fumes. But this vehicle appeared to a steady and tough one, at least. Not a rusty bucket of loose metals as Shyambabu's vehicle was. A cry from Shyambabu caught his attention. He was calling them to get into the jeep. He was ready to start.

It was absolutely dark all around. The twin lances of head-lights speared the darkness as they purred along. Satrajit was dead tired after all the hectic operating and things and he began to doze. Suddenly there was a cough, then a splutter, then the engine died off altogether.

"Now what, Shyambabu?" Satrajit asked hoarsely. Shyambabu took out his torch from the glove compartment and smiled.

"Sir, you worry too much. Don't fret please. There is nothing that Shyam can't set straight. Depend upon me, Sir." His smile was so disarming that Satrajit could not say anything. Moreover, what was to be said? They were stranded here, in the middle of nowhere, at the mercy of this man and the vehicle that he ran. No one understood the jeep better than Shyambabu. He had been driving it for ages now.

The hood had been pushed up with Shyambabu bent low over the engine, muttering curses under his breath. Satrajit waited for a reasonable time and then alighted from his seat to inspect the extent of damage. He knew nothing about engines, but sitting idle, doing nothing, was more than he could bear.

This time Shyambabu appeared to be far from his usual reassuring self. He was sombre pulling a long face.

"Sir, extremely bad news!" He was dramatic in his declaration.

"What is it?" Satrajit asked.

"I'll be damned if I knew! Sorry, Sir, please excuse my bad language."

"No, that's alright. But, you mean to say that you don't know what's ailing this monster?"

"He has grown old Sir, with a whole lot of geriatric problems." Years in the Government Health Service made Shyambabu use medical jargons under duress. "This is a case of multi-system failure. How can I set it right in a trice? He needs to be hospitalized!"

Satrajit walked a few paces away to take in the surroundings. There was nothing much to take in, actually. The entire area was dark. Electricity had not made much of headway in these parts. The pale sliver of a moon hanging listless in a clear sky, threw more shadows than light. The tall conifers all around, amidst dense undergrowth appeared sinister. This was bear country – home to the Himalayan black bear. All cases of mauling by bears rushed through Satrajit's mind like a sanguineous slideshow. But, of course, he told himself, winter was setting in. So, all bears must be deep in their slumber. But who knows? Maybe there were some who suffered from insomnia! He turned back to address Shyambabu.

"So, what do we do, Shyambabu? What do you suggest? Should we wait out here or move to some other place?"

"Sir, I think there is no point in waiting. If you walk downhill along this road, you will reach Latpanchor in a short while. Something can be done there. I mean some vehicle can be arranged."

"How far is Latpanchor from here?"

"I am not very sure, Sir. To my reckoning it should not be more than two kilometres from here...or maybe three."

Satrajit mused. There was really no point in sitting out here, in the wilderness, in the middle of nowhere. At least the village of Latpanchor was known to him. The Cinchona Plantation Hospital had a vehicle. Surely they could get a lift as far as Sukna, where something could be done. He looked up. Streaks of fire danced in a far away hill. The undergrowth was being burnt to leave the soil richer. Probably a tea garden out there, somewhere. He called to his teammates. They were all looking up at him, waiting for his guidance.

They decided to walk over to Latpanchor and try their luck after they reached that village. So, on they moved, in a single file down the road. Shyambabu was not ready to abandon his vehicle and said that he would stay there, guarding the jeep, and waiting for some help. But he was not ready to part with his torch. Now, the only hope of the surgical team was the puny pencil torch that Satrajit always carried with him.

They moved on in silence. All were pretty tense, but none more than Akshay, the Anaesthetist. Prem, the OT attendant, was panting. His was the most arduous job as he had to lug the heavy case containing the laparoscope and accessories. The incessantly chattering Nursing Staff were muted, for a change. Satrajit led the way, his briefcase in his left hand and the glowworm of a torch in his right.

A pair of eyes glowed in a roadside bush, in the wash of the light from the torch. They were burning red. Satrajit, who was walking ahead of the rest, noticed it first and came to a sudden stop. All of them stared at the eyes, petrified in terror. Akshay stammered, "B-a-a-gh...". Tiger, he meant. Satrajit shooed him shut. He had his doubt. Had it been one of the big cats, why was it so low down in the bush? Why had it not attacked? Of course, a tiger was out of the question. There was none in the jungles out here, but a leopard could be a possibility, crouching low, waiting to pounce on its unsuspecting victims. Gently Satrajit moved his light to where the eyes were glowing. In total silence an animal broke cover and leapt down the side of the hill that sloped down towards the gorge to their left, and disappeared. Satrajit's cry of relief echoed from the dark, rolling hills all around. A pair of long ears and a bobbing tail had told him that it was a hare, probably more frightened than they were. A night bird flapped its wings and screeched in fright at the laughter, to fly soundlessly away. The team plodded on once again.

"Now, everybody, keep your weather eyes open." Satrajit cautioned. "In the darkness we may pass through the Latpanchor village, not even knowing that we have left it behind us. There is no other human habitation beyond that."

Even as he spoke, houses loomed up ahead of them, dark smudges in the dark environment. One of them showed a glimmer of lantern through a partially open window.

"Sister," called Satrajit. "Will you please go up to the window and ask the lady I can see from here, about how far Latpanchor is from here?" The Nurse went up to the house, while the others waited. She came back with a wide grin.

"Sir, we have reached Latpanchor."

Now they measured their steps with new found confidence. About two hundred metres along the road they came upon a crossing. Just beyond this place was the hospital. Satrajit asked the others to wait under an awning in front of a closed shop and went over to the hospital, along with Prem.

A shock awaited them. The pharmacist recognized Satrajit. He was courtesy personified, but said that so sorry, the doctor of this hospital had taken the only vehicle they had and gone over to Siliguri and he wouldn't be coming back before the next morning but would they please come into his quarters and have some refreshments. Satrajit politely declined this magnanimous offer and walked over to where the others waited in eager expectation. Prem waved his hands at them from afar and called out, "They are not there." Akshay slumped.

Now, they had no way out, but to wait. Ten at night in this part of the hills sans electricity, was what midnight was in the bigger towns like Kurseong. Not a soul stirred. As if to torment them further, a wind, chilling to the bones, rose. Fingers of a mountain mist began to curl in. The watches ticked on.

An hour's patient waiting paid off in the end. High above in the hills they had been travelling down, a pair of headlights lanced the dark wall. It wound down, coming towards them.

Prem and Satrajit went up to stand in the middle of the road. This was their last hope and they were not ready to let it slip away.

"There they are." someone shouted. It was the other jeep belonging to the Health Centre, now ferrying the staff and doctors of the Health Centre, home.

"I am sorry, Sir. I am really sorry." Kishen Daju apologized. "But just see for yourself, Sir, not a single square inch is vacant in this jeep. Where can I accommodate you?"

"But, Daju, something has to be done!"

"Wait, Sir, I have a better idea. I know a driver who's from this village and who has a cab for hire. Maybe his vehicle is free right now. Please let me go and check him out."

Kishen Daju went off with a purpose. The wait seemed very long. But this time it was different. People alighted from the jeep and began chatting with the stranded ones. Soon all discussion livened up and drove the cobwebs of monotony and tension away.

A pair of headlights bobbed over the uneven road, rather like the stern lights of a steamer. Kishen Daju was leaning out of the passenger side window yelling and waving. Their ordeal had come to an end.

The car they had hired at Latpanchor dropped them off at the Sukna Health Centre. Kishen Daju, after a hurried dinner, picked them up in his jeep to drop them home at Kurseong. The only snag was that all telephones in Sukna were dead, so they could not let Kurseong know that they were safe.

"What of Shyambabu?" Satrajit asked Kishen.

"What of him?"

"I mean where is he now? What will he do?"

"He is still there, where you had left him, guarding his ramshackle jeep. A team will go from Siliguri in the morning to tow him down. Till then he has to sit tight. If we are lucky maybe the elephants will find him before our team does!" Kishen Daju's guffaw sent sleeping crows flying all around.

A red signal stopped them just before they were about to enter the sleeping town of Kurseong. A police cordon stopped their jeep.

"Is the Doctor Saab with you?" A disembodied voice asked from the dark roadside. Then a man in the uniform of a police officer loomed into vision.

"Yes," replied Satrajit. "Here I am."

"Sir, you are under arrest. Please come over to our jeep."

An astounded Satrajit alighted from his jeep and moved over to the police vehicle.

"What is it officer? What have I done?"

Then the officer moved into the area lit up by the headlights. He was grinning from ear to ear. He was very well known to Satrajit.

"Mokhtan! It's you? Hey, what's up?" asked Satrajit.

"Ha ha, Doc, caught you, haven't I? It's nothing, actually. Just that you have to make a brief stop on the way, at my quarters. Don't worry, my men will go over to your place and tell Bhabhi that you are back. Do you know that seeing that you people have not returned from camp till midnight she got so worried that she made Dr. Roy inform our Control Room Sukna P.S. has been alerted through a radio message and a search party was ready to leave for Ranglitar? Telephones in Sukna are out since evening. Luckily the Sukna people had come to know that you have already left Sukna and were on your way back. So I put together this reception in your honour."

"All that's fine," said Satrajit, "but what about this brief stop thing?"

"Nothing much Doc. my wife is having a tummy ache since dinner. As you'll be going the same way, I thought that it will be better if you just saw her before you went." Mrs. Mokhtan was an old patient of Satrajit. Satrajit sighed and shrugged. It had been a long day, but a tummy ache is a tummy ache.

Satrajit swept his eyes over the town ahead of him. It was dark, with only a few street lights burning. The sodium vapour lamps along the Hill Cart Road curved up ahead like a bride's necklace. All houses were dark. Kurseong was sleeping. In the eyes of his mind he could see only one house well lit-up like a Christmas tree, with a pair of eyes keeping vigil from the bedroom window, as the little one slept. Satrajit turned to Mokhtan.

"Well Cavalryman, lead the way."

✦ ✦ ✦

14

The Charioteer

Rome was asleep. It was past midnight. One by one all the lamps were extinguished plunging the city in darkness. A pale moon hung limply in the sky accentuating the darkness of the shadows cast. The elongated strip of wavering light prostrated upon the road outside the public drinking house was an island in the dark sea. Drunken songs wafted out occasionally to stir the still night air. The city slept.

Only two persons, apart from the patrons of the public house, were awake. One was a patrician and the other nobody. But both stayed awake because of the same reason.

Pontius Claudius, the patrician, lay in luxury, on his sprawling four-poster, staring at the billowing white silk curtains, laced with gold. His wife was away. His mistress lay curled on her side, nude under her white silk covers. The woman mumbled in her sleep and snuggled closer. Claudius pushed her off and went up to the window, wrapping a toga around him. Outside, the city slept like a spent lover. Out there, somewhere, his dream was being squandered. His *quadriga* – chariot drawn by four horses – would not run in the race on Jupiter's Day.

The horses snorted. All of them loved Gaius, the lanky young man, of Thracian descent. Gaius was a slave in the household of Pontius Claudius. From a very young age he had been taking care of horses. He loved horses and chariot racing. Recently, for about a year or so, he had been directly involved with racing. Only a few months ago he had driven his owner's team to victory on his debut race and had been acclaimed in racing circuits as a prodigy. All said that he was the rising star in the *Veneti factiones,* to which his owner's team belonged. There were four *factiones, Prasini* (the Greens), *Russata* (the Reds), *Albata* (the Whites) and his own *faction, Veneti* (the Aquamarines). The *Prasini* and the *Veneti* were the most high profile *factiones*. Whenever they encountered each other on the racing tracks, tension ran high.

Gaius had won three races in a row. His owner had been so happy that he had declared that if Gaius won the next race, he would be given his freedom and would continue racing as a salaried freeman. That big event was to begin in a day from now, but a misfortune was keeping him awake.

Gaius roamed about aimlessly in the darkened stables. He went over to the stall where his team of race horses stood. He leaned against the post of the first stall and absently stroked the silken neck of the horse there. The horse snorted in pleasure.

"Andremone," Gaius murmured, calling the horse by his name. "We are desolate. Where could he have gone? Ah, I wish you could talk!" The horse nuzzled up to him, as if to offer his consolation.

The 'awesome foursome' they were called in the racing circuits – the black quartet of Pontius Claudius' Aquamarine *quadriga* team. All were from the same litter and almost identical in appearance, jet black in colour with a white streak on their foreheads. Lovingly they were named Andremone, Musculosus, Piripinus and Calimorfus. Amongst these four, Calimorfus, as the *funalis*, was the key member and pilot for the other horses. He functioned as the pivot during the short and sharp turn at the turning points in the course or *metae*.

Calimorfus, affectionately known as Cali, was missing for four days now. Without him the *quadriga* meant nothing. No replacement could be found or trained at such short notice. This shocking news had been carefully kept under wraps so far. Any spillage would spell out disaster and riots. Gaius used to sleep in the stable that housed the racing steeds. Even then Calimorfus had gone missing. Claudius had issued an ultimatum to Gaius.

"If that horse does not run on the day of the festival of Jupiter, then, by the name of all gods, I'll flay you alive!"

At daybreak the pensive and forlorn Gaius trudged out of the gates of the Claudius hacienda. The morning was bright, the grass green and birds were chirping in the orange trees. Outside the huge iron gates, Rome was awash in the golden light of the morning sun. But all this glory was wasted on the young man, for nothing seems right to a heart heavy with grief and anxiety. Even more than his own well being, the thoughts that ate into him were what was Cali doing? Had he eaten? How was he? There was no doubt that he had been stolen. But who was responsible and how had it been possible? ...unless... He drove the thought out of his mind. How could it be an inside job? All loved Cali and the team. All were eager to see them romp home, victorious. Then?

Gaius' feet carried him over to the Circus Maximus, the venue of the next day's chariot racing. A sizable crowd was assembled outside the Circus, in spite of the early hour. Traders yelled themselves hoarse, peddling their fare. Shops had opened up, selling fruits, flowers, leather goods and such other oddities of household use. Far to his right, a blacksmith was doing steady business, shoeing horses and making swords and other weapons. Next to him a carpenter was busy filing a beam into silky smoothness.

Suddenly someone bumped into Gaius. He turned to see a pair of beautiful eyes fluttering at him. Slender, white arms reached out at him and dainty fingers held his calloused hands fast. The girl smiled at him as she placed one of his hands on her young breasts.

"Feel them, my love! Take them as you please." whispered the girl. A prostitute! She, too, was busy peddling her fare. Gaius shrank back.

"I am an ordinary slave! I can't afford you. Please find someone else." he said in alarm.

"I know what you are. I also know who you are. You are Gaius, the Charioteer. I love to see you racing in this Circus. I hope you win tomorrow."

"Who knows?" Gaius sighed. Probably he would not be racing at all tomorrow.

"Are you sad? Is anything the matter?"

"No. Nothing. Why should it?" Gaius asked.

The girl sighed and moved away. She stood still for a while. Then furtively, she looked about her and said.

"I hear things. I know things. Meet me, my dear. Meet me after the sun has crossed the zenith, in the woods beyond the Palatine Hills. I shall tell you what I know." She smiled as she melted away in the crowd.

Gaius sighed, shook his head, and entered the Circus Maximus. Some charioteers were already there, training their teams and getting the measure of the course. Newly constructed marble stands for the spectators sparkled in the morning sun. The Emperor Trajan had been gracious enough to build them with marble after a devastating fire had destroyed the old wooden stands. Statues of Jupiter, Neptune, Apollo and Diana adorned the *spinae* – the dividing six feet high wall. Tall obelixes marked the *metae.* Gaius' fingers twitched in an urge to hold the reins. The glorious morning beckoned him. Step by step he went up ahead to stand right at the edge of the racing tracks.

Three teams were hard at practice this morning. Maybe others would come in later. Amongst the three, the *quadriga* of chestnut horses caught his eyes. He knew this team. It belonged to a middle aged patrician, a war hero, called Pius Antonius. Antonius had his palatial establishment near the Forum, at the heart of Rome. This was their ancestral home. He also had a villa far away from the crowded city, where he went every now and then to shake off all the grime of city life

The chestnut team was good, very good. Gaius knew the charioteer. He was a villainous looking ruffian, a freeman called Scipio, after the great Roman general. He was better known by his nickname, Scorpio, for his sting was as bad as his looks. An utterly unscrupulous charioteer, he often slashed other charioteers with his whip or dashed into others on purpose. He rode for the *Prasini factiones* (the Greens).

Scipio noticed Gaius standing there, disconsolate, as he rounded the far *meta*. He reined in his horses as he neared the younger man.

"What ho, dear Gaius? Not in practice today? Or will you come in later?" asked he. "Or perhaps you are not competing this time, eh?"

Gaius looked up sharply at his most vicious opponent in the tracks.

"Don't you dare give me the looks, you whippersnapper, I know what you know and I also know what you don't know!" With that he burst into a vicious guffaw and set his team galloping with a violent crack of his whip. Gaius stood there for a while, mulling on what he had just heard, then, finding no answer, traced his steps homeward. A lot remained to be done at the stables.

Gaius was fortunate in that not much intellect was needed in the daily chores at the stables. He cleaned the stalls, replenished the hay and fodder, gave the horses a rub down, and polished the tacks. He did all this mechanically. In his mind he was seeking an answer to the riddle that the Scorpio had posed. He could not make any head or tail of it. Who stood to gain if Cali did not run? The Greens, of course, and that meant the Scorpio! But why should he give any lead in the matter of Cali being unable to run if he had been directly involved? What if he was not directly involved? Then was there anyone else who could be involved? Antonius? But how could a war hero stoop so low? Anyway, things ought to get somewhat clear by the afternoon. He recalled his encounter with the prostitute. Perhaps she really knew something. He shelved this line of thought aside and changed tracks. In his mind began to run over all that had passed that fateful night.

That night, Gaius was very tired. A strenuous workout with the horses under the watchful eyes of his master had taken its toll. He had planned to retire early. Veronica, the slave girl, assigned to him, had come up with food. Now, this girl was something. Full of bouncy energy, she took care of him well enough and was extremely proficient in bed. Gaius remembered the day when his mistress, Lucia, had first assigned her to his care. Veronica had been Lucia's personal maid, and she still was.

It was the night after the first victory. There were celebrations galore at the hacienda. Wine flowed like water and food was abundant. There was plenty of singing and dancing too, as this was the first victory run of his master. Gaius had been the centre of attention and he, too, had a little bit to drink. His master, with his cronies, was soon sprawled on the cushions scattered around, and all were totally soused. It was near midnight, when the revellers began to fall asleep one after the another and the minstrels had gone hoarse with constant singing. Lucia, the mistress, herself in quite an inebriated state, had stood up and had proceeded towards her bedchamber. She did not sleep with Claudius, but had her own chamber for quite some time now. On her way she had stopped and murmured some instructions in the ears of her personal maid, Anastasia.

Gaius looked about him in wonder. In his long stint at the hacienda he had never before stepped inside the sanctum of the first lady's personal chamber. By the time Gaius had entered the room, Lady Lucia had already changed into a loose fitting, flimsy, night gown. She smiled at Gaius as he entered and beckoned him to come forward.

"So, boy wonder! How you have grown! Now you are a man! Here, come closer. Let me take a look at you."

At Lucia's behest, Gaius' purple cloak was unclasped at the neck and removed. Next Anastasia came up to remove his loin cloth and he stood there completely in the nude, acutely embarrassed. Lucia ran her appreciative glance all over his body.

"My, my!" she said. "You have really become a man! Just look, Anastasia, isn't he wonderful?" Lucia's laughter jingled like a chandelier shattering to pieces. "He needs to be taken care of." She signalled with a jerk of her head and a girl entered the room.

"Veronica," she ordered. "Gaius is our precious possession. Take care of him in every way. I am sure you know how to do it all."

Thus Veronica wove a net around Gaius' night life. Every night she brought him his food, not the regular repast that the slaves had, but wholesome, nourishing stuff, and after that made love to him. She did not stay back, though. After making love she left, taking away the used utensils. A bondage had sprung up between them. It was nowhere near love. But was more base, more carnal.

They had not made love that night. Gaius had felt unaccountably sleepy. He seemed to have blacked out shortly after eating. When he awoke the next morning, he found that the stable door was wide open, the wicker gate of the stalls, unlatched and Calimorfus gone. As he made an attempt to stand up, he had to catch hold of the stall-rail. His head was spinning and he had a king sized headache. He stumbled against something, which rolled away with a clatter. A pitcher! Empty! But when had he drunk?

Claudius was livid! He accused Gaius of dereliction of duty and had him flogged, tying him to a post out there in the garden. Gaius bore it all. Incredulity at the loss of Cali, the horse he had loved most, together with the impassive expression that he had seen on Veronica's face while he was being flogged, had served to benumb him. Claudius had stopped after the fifth stroke saying that he needed him intact for the races and that Gaius was to find the horse for him. He had pronounced his ultimatum thereafter.

There was almost no shadow under his feet. The sun was directly overhead. Gaius' tired feet carried him beyond the Palatine Hills, into the woods. He had given up the hope of seeing his friend, old Calimorfus, ever again. Standing in the woods, he looked about him. At first he could see no one. Then a glimmer of white came into view within the lattice-work of light and shade. The girl smiled at him. She caught his hand and made him sit beside her on a grass bank.

"Don't be so sad and empty, dear Gaius, this day will be something you'd remember as long as you live," said the girl. Then with a fleeting smile she added, "I am called Galina, if you are interested."

Gaius slumped there, sad and dejected. His whole world was crashing down upon him.

"Come to me, Gaius," Galina called. Gaius looked up at her. Slowly, ever so slowly, she took off her tunic. She stood there, looking just like the embodiment of Venus.

"Take me, my love, I yearn for you."

Later, totally spent, but satiated, they lay side by side on the grass bank. The sun played hide and seek with them through the leaves of the tree overhead. Galina sat up."For the first time in my life I have offered myself with love. You gave me something in return which no one had ever given me before. You have treated me with respect. You have treated me as a woman. Now, I will tell you something that will change your world.

I have seen your horse, the black one with a white marking on his forehead."

Gaius sat up, instantly alert.

"Where have you seen him? When?"

"In the country house of Pius Antonius." Gaius took a sharp breath. Galina raised her hand to cut him off. "Two nights ago, there were festivities in the country house. My service was enlisted as a serving girl and other entertainments. There I heard that they were celebrating their victory on Jupiter's Day, in anticipation. I heard certain remarks that made me suspicious. I was sure that your horse has been stolen and is hidden out there in the grounds somewhere. Later I went out into the grounds on some pretext. Far away, behind a clump of bushes I heard the snorting of a horse. I gave a low whistle and he whinnied in response." Gaius jumped up and began putting on his clothes.

"Where are you going?" asked Galina.

"Why? To Antonius' country house, of course!"

"Are you mad?" Galina pulled him down. "The guards will cut you into pieces and feed them to the dogs! Sit still. I have a plan for you."

The night was dark and hazy. A dark, shadowy figure crept up the slope of the Palatine Hills, walking a horse behind him. It was past midnight, so nobody was around. As he went over to the far side, a hushed hissing sound was heard. The shadow stopped in his path. Another shadow materialized from the trees to join him. Now both of them vaulted to the back of the horse and galloped away, the sounds of the hoof beats effectively muzzled by the thick stockings of jute wound round the horse's hooves. The shadows in black and the black horse with no tell tale pale areas simply melted into the darkness.

Gaius, for it was he, was well armed with a short sword used by legionaries and gladiators, known as the Gladius and a small but deadly dagger, known as the Pugio. He was attired in the full regalia of a charioteer, complete with a leather helmet, leather arm and shin guards and knee pads. His aquamarine, full sleeved *vestis quadrigaria*, covered by a corset of leather bands, was camouflaged by a black cloak. Galina was less encumbered, just wrapping a black mantle over her black tunic. She also had a pugio tucked in her waist band just in case. In her left hand Galina held on tightly to a small bag containing dog food. Off they galloped towards the villa of Pius Antonius at top speed.

Before leaving the hacienda, Gaius had some specific instructions for the team of seven slaves who worked in the stable and in the grounds. They were to take the rest of the *quadriga*, fully readied, to the Circus Maximus in the early hours of the next morning. They were to answer no question regarding the whereabouts of Gaius, or the black stallion from their stable.

Gaius dropped out of sight at the foot of the villa wall. A well branched ancient tree was there, spreading its branches over the wall itself. Gaius shinnied up this tree, while Galina tied the horse to one of its lower branches. When Gaius had reached up to the level of the wall, Galina threw the bag of dog-feed up at him, which he caught dextrously. Next Galina followed him up. Gaius vaulted down and looked about him, on the alert, gladius drawn. Galina landed softly beside him, with the merest whisper of a sound. Then they waited with bated breaths. They, however, did not have to wait for too long. Soon hoarse panting could be heard. Dogs were coming for them. Galina calmly took out the chunks of beef and offal she had been carrying in her bag and tossed them in the direction of the speeding canine guards. The dogs pounced on the meat without paying the intruders any attention. One by one they stumbled and fell over silently. The meat was drugged and the first hurdle was crossed.

While Gaius tiptoed over towards the direction where Calimorfus was supposed to be, Galina ran on towards the main gate. She knew that there would be two sentries on duty. Sentries they were, to be sure, but they were men, after all. Soon enough, murmurs were heard from the direction of the gates. Gaius hurried forward. He had to skirt the single-storied building to go to the far side, where Calimorfus was sequestered. While passing under the open window of the house, Gaius heard voices and froze. Not voices, exactly, but moaning of lust. The woman's voice was so familiar that Gaius could not help peep inside. His heart also leapt out of his throat. She was the mistress of his master, Lucia, in bed, with Antonius. So he was her paramour! Lucia propped herself up ran her finger down Antonius' chest.

"When you win tomorrow dear, it will be due to me. Remember that. I had arranged for everything. There's nothing I won't do for you, my love!"

Gaius moved away stealthily. He had seen and heard more than was good for him. He swallowed hard to control the gush of bile running up his throat and sped away.

Calimorfus was agitated on seeing his friend and master. Gaius calmed him down, gave him the lump of sugar he had brought for him and unhitched his stay. Then he walked him off towards the gate.

Galina was lying in the arms of one of the sentries, while the other man was sitting bemused. He never saw the shadowy figure creep up to him from behind. The gladius cut across his throat at the same time Galina's pugio buried itself under the left ribcage of the other one. Both died without a sound. Galina was splattered with blood. She wiped herself dry on the guard's tunic and vaulted over Calimorfus' back, her own tunic bundled up under her arm.

They changed horses at the bottom of the large tree, where Galina made herself presentable. Then off they went like whirlwind.

The eastern sky was blushing like a new bride and the sun was rising in all its splendour as they climbed up the final crest of hills. Rome lay beneath them, eagerly waiting for the day's festivities to begin. Far away they could make out the procession winding its way from the Capitol and passing through the Forum, to the trill of trumpets and beat of drums. The chariots of the gods could be made out. The largest was, of course Jupiter's. Then there were those of the Dioscuri Twins, Cibele, the mother of the gods and Neptune, the god of horses. They rode down at breakneck speed, heading straight for the Circus. Near the Circus, they parted way. Gaius went directly towards the *porta Triumphalis* – the triumphal gate – in order to enter much ahead of the procession itself. While Galina wheeled her mount towards the Claudius hacienda. There she left the black horse at the gate. The horse dutifully trotted in and headed towards his own stall in the stables.

The jostling crowd, gathered in front of the *porta Triumphalis,* the main entrance to the huge Circus Maximus, scattered as Calimorfus thundered in. The usual din of a holiday crowd was silenced for a while. Then it broke into an expectant chatter. A juggler missed the balls tossed up and they went bouncing away in all directions. The street urchins had a field day.

Calimorfus needed no directions. He knew the way well enough. With unerring precision he headed straight for the flat end of the circus known as *officium,* where the *carceres* or stables were located.

The six support staff of the *Veneti* team of Claudius, were a dejected lot. They had worked mechanically getting the other three horses ready, along with the racing chariot, but they did not have their heart in their actions. Calimorfus' absence had broken their hearts. They knew that Gaius would not return. They knew that this team would not run.

By daybreak the news of Cali's absence had spread like wildfire. The bookies were devastated and so were the larger number of the *Veneti* supporters. They had another team from their *faction,* no doubt, but Gaius was Gaius! The *Prasini* supporters, on the other hand, began pruning their feathers like haughty cockerels. The lead charioteer, Scipio the Scorpio, was seen hovering around with a smug smile, twirling the whip in his hand.

An uproar rose from the stands. The curious staff of Claudius ran out to see what was wrong. A black horse with a white streak on his forehead was thundering down the tracks. Bent low over his back was a known figure in Aquamarine uniform! "Calimorfus"! Their cry sounded like a battle cry above all din! The procession entered the Circus through the *porta Triumphalis*.

Trumpets trilled and bugles blared. The dignitaries came in one by one to take their designated seats in the stands. The trumpets sounded once again. All rose from their seats. The columns of the Praetorian Guards presented arms. The Emperor Trajan entered with his entourage amidst chants of "Caesar, Caesar." The Emperor raised his right hand. Instantaneous silence reigned. Trajan took his seat in the Imperial Box, the *pulvinor*.

With the roll of drums and the blowing of trumpets the chariots rolled in one by one, to take up their designated slots at the starting line. The crowds yelled their heads off. A herald announced the names of the charioteer and the owner. The charioteers raised his whip-hand in salute to the Emperor. The spectators shouted themselves hoarse.

But all the shouts were nothing compared to the welcome that Gaius received. There was one figure in the patrician stands that yelled as much as any plebeian. Pontius Claudius was ecstatic! But the seat to his left was vacant, as was an important chair to the left of the Emperor. Gaius was unmoved by all this. He stood in his chariot, erect like a god and as handsome. His calm visage did not show any sign of tiredness. He held the reins in an iron grip and in his right hand he held his whip in utter nonchalance. He never needed to use it. He controlled his horses with a touch of reins and loving, verbal commands. His whip was for self protection against assaults from other charioteers less scrupulous than him.

Gaius' eyes roved. They roamed over the stands searching for someone in the crowds. Galina was jumping up and down in excitement. But Gaius could not find her in the teeming populace.

The Emperor's handkerchief or *mappa* fell. Amidst thunderous roar from the thousands of voices drowning out the trumpets, the full seven lap race began. Chariots trundled, hooves thundered and charioteers began blazing the trail! Soon began the disasters. Chariots crashed into each other, horses got tangled and fell with flailing limbs. Heads got bashed. By the time the fourth metal dolphin dipped his head in the lap counter, two men were dead and four, maimed for life.

The awesome foursome lived up to their reputation. They were indeed awesome and Calimorfus surpassed himself in speed, agility, reflex and guile. Gaius raced with only one purpose in mind. From the very first turn, he shot in the lead and he maintained this position all through. He raced with such a single minded concentration that even the Scorpio could not reach him within whip length. His romping home by more than a horse's length was a dramatic anticlimax. The crowd went berserk!

Gaius dragged his feet homewards, twirling his all important laurel wreath in his hand. A slave had emerged last night, a freeman was returning. Galina was waiting for him. She ran up to embrace him. He stood there with his head on her shoulder.

"Galina, I am so tired. Will you take care of me please?" he asked.

"I will, my love, I will."

"Always?"

"Always."

The story has been previously published online in 'Your Story Club' in June 2012. Ancient Rome section of mariamilani.com was used besides Wikipedia for description of the locale, the racing events, uniforms and equipments.

✦ ✦ ✦

15

A Sweet Arrangement

Kolkata was throwing fits. A freak decision by the local government had the city convulsing. All milk products were banned. The Government had felt that babies were being deprived of the milk they deserved, and most of the available milk was being converted to milk products like sandesh, rosogolla and other sweets, along with curd, cheese, cottage cheese and the like. But Bengalis were known for their sweet tooth. Moreover, the sandesh and rosogolla gave a sort of identity to the people. Therefore, Kolkata, and subsequently Bengal, convulsed. "Why is the milk production not being increased?" This was the question being asked in trams, buses, coffee houses, in short everywhere. But the ban remained in place and Kolkatans suffered. They had to make do with poor substitutes like *besan* or gram flour, sweet potato and other such things. Heaps of laddus of various hues and sizes got a sudden break and found places of prominence in the showcases of renowned confectioners. The situation was ridiculous. It was in the early 1960s. Kolkatans would long remember those days of woe.

Bilupishi was a dear. Youngest amongst the siblings of my father, she had been widowed for a long time... I had never seen her husband but heard many tales about him. He was an intrepid Forest Officer, I think they were called Rangers those days, but I might be mistaken. He was responsible for the arrest of many criminals who had been stealing timber from the forests of North Bengal and from what I heard, one day he did not come back home. He had been killed. Why or how I did not know. I was too young to understand. But that is beside the point. The point is that Bilupishi had stayed back at Siliguri and used to come home to Kolkata only once in a while. She had been very fond of me and whenever she visited us she had a parting gift for me when she left. This time, it was a crisp five rupee note.

In those days five rupees could buy many things. So I was as happy as a prince and could not rest till it was spent.

"Tridib, what can you buy with a five rupee note?" Tridib was my closest friend in our locality that we called Para. He scratched his head and gaped. Really! I have never seen a dumber buffoon in my life.

"Let's have some salted peanuts."

Just look at him! This was all he could suggest! With five rupees we could buy peanuts to last us a month maybe. This will not do. So I put my foot down.

"Leave it," said I. "I'll think of something later."

The summer vacation had started. It was fun galore. After the homework was completed we used to rush over to the playground every morning and played football. This was life!

But, in spite of all the fun, one thing kept gnawing at me – the unspent five rupee note. At last I could bear it no longer.

One morning, after the football match was over and all the participants had departed, I called Tridib over. With both hands in the pockets of my trousers, I sauntered about with an air of feigned nonchalance.

"I am going over to the main road. Care to come?"

"But what for?" asked Tridib.

"I'll spend some of the money I have with me."

"Now?" Really this chap could provoke you to a fit of frustrated rage!

"Then?" I asked in response. "When do you want this money to be spent? On the day of your wedding?"

Left with no option, Tridib had to come with me to the main road.

It was well near noon and the blazing sun ensured that people stayed indoors. The asphalt was showing signs of melting. An ice cream vendor was standing in a tiny shade and fanning himself ineffectually with a towel, by which, at intervals he wiped his face. Now, at long last, Tridib made the first intelligent observation.

"Look," he cried, "an ice cream cart!"

"Yes, I can see that."

"Let's...!" He swallowed the rest of the sentence as his mouth had begun watering.

I grinned. "Ok, let's go."

An ice cream on a hot summer day works wonders with half asleep brain cells. Tridib swallowed the last piece on his cone and gulped.

"Let's have some sweets, shall we?" I agreed instantly.

Netaida's shop was the best in the neighbourhood. We made a beeline for this shop. It was more or less deserted. Only a few customers were there. It seemed as if business had not picked up that day. We looked at the showcase and there was not a single item that excited our imagination. With a long face we stepped away from the shop debating on what to do next, when someone called out. It could hardly qualify for a call, as it simply said, "Pssst...hey!" but it was enough to draw our attention. There, on the opposite footpath stood Netaida. He was calling us frantically. We crossed over to where he stood. Netaida, put his finger on his lips and called us to the nearest by lane. With a conspiratorial air, he looked first to his right, then to his left and finally whispered in a sepulchral tone.

"Want to taste some rosogolla or sandesh?"

We simply could not believe our ears. Rosogolla! Sandesh! What was he saying? It was as if he was ready to get some manna from the Heaven for us.

"Oh yes!" We replied in chorus.

"Then, come! But mind it; the cost will be four times higher than the usual one."

Tridib looked at me with a bit of uncertainty. But I puffed out my chest like an intrepid Musketeer. I had recently read the novel by Dumas in an abridged form and was still full of it.

We followed good old Netaida down the lane, turned right into the first by lane, turned right yet again and found ourselves in the rear entrance of a big house. At first we could not make out where we were. But soon recognition dawned. It was the house of the confectioner himself. Netaida called us in through the rear entrance. We went in through a dingy passage that opened into a large kitchen. This was Netaida's reserve 'factory' that he pressed into service on the event of fulfilling large pending commitments. Netaida dived under a low shelf to drag out two large containers. From one, he took out four rosogollas for each of us and from the other, two sandesh each. He put the rosogollas in an earthenware cup and the sandesh in a paper packet. Then he pocketed the money I offered, but cautioned us in a hard note.

"Don't you dare tell anyone that I had given you sweets. Finish them off right now and throw the used cups in that bin and shut the door behind you before you go." With that, he left.

Looking at each other, with eyes glittering in joy, we finished the rosogollas in a trice. Then we decided to eat the sandesh at a leisurely pace in some better place. This place was too dingy for comfort with a weird smell.

Tridib was a glutton. He could hardly restrain himself. As soon as we reached the main road he took out his packet from his pocket and took a nibble, shooting a glance in my direction. I was thinking of the five rupee note I had spent this morning. Had it been worthwhile? I thought. Then absently, I too took my packet out and started to nibble the sandesh.

The villainous grip on the scruff of our neck almost made us leap out of our own skins. We turned back to see a huge policeman, of a towering stature, a moustache and protruding tummy to match at us. He had put his baton under his armpit to ensure that his hands were free.

"Huh! So what are you eating my boys?" He asked. A pointless question really, for he could very well see that we were eating sandesh. He would not have bothered to look at us even had we been chewing coconuts.

"So, you won't tell me, will you?" How could we? Our mouths were full!

"All right. Come with me to the police station." This was too much.

"You won't? Then show me where you got these sweets from."

"Then will you let us go?" My voice trembled even as I asked the question.

"Yes, I promise, but only after you show me the place."

We led the policeman through the lane and by lanes till we came to the backyard of Netaida and silently pointed out the den of crime for his benefit.

"Ok," the policeman nodded with satisfaction. "Now go. Don't hang around here anymore." With this he marched straight towards the entrance, now shut and apparently bolted from the inside, and rapped with his baton, crying, "Open up!" in his most officious tone. The door opened instantaneously, as if by magic and poor Netaida, trembling from head to foot, stepped out. The policeman gestured with his baton and both of them stepped across the threshold and disappeared.

We were too flabbergasted to move. We stood rooted to the spot for a while. Thereafter, we ducked behind the broken down wall to wait.

It was a long wait for us. Ultimately the door opened and the policeman and Netaida came out together laughing at some joke. The policeman was wiping his mouth with his hand. Netaida asked him to wait and went back to bring a glass of water. The policeman took a long, cool drink, rinsed his mouth, spat the water out into the ground nearby and washed his hand, before handing the glass tumbler back to

Netaida. After that he took out a large, dirty handkerchief from his trouser pocket and while wiping his hand, told Netaida, belching.

"Your sweets are very tasty, Mr. Modak. Tomorrow I'd like to taste some rajbhog and rosomalai the day after."

A visibly relieved Netaida bent his head over his shoulder in agreement, a huge smile lighting up his oily countenance. It was a sweet arrangement indeed!

✦ ✦ ✦

16

Walker on a Wet Street

"Here day is night and night is day. Just take a look outside your windows and then look at your watch, you'll understand what I mean to say." The guide, a young man of about twenty odd years, smiled. He had told them that his name was Jimmy when he had met them at the Bangkok Airport. His real name was something unpronounceable, and so he had shortened it into 'Jimmy' for the convenience of the tourists he served, a name every tongue would be able to pronounce.

This was his first trip to Thailand. In fact, this was his first trip to any foreign country. Shivam was an editor in a local newspaper, who wasted his time writing. He wrote on everything under the sun, even on matters that did not concern him. He wrote essays, short and long stories, a few novels too, but the worst thing about him was that he wrote poetry. No harm in that either. The only problem was that, unlike many who wrote poems, he was a real poet. He wrote well and even at heart he was a poet that many others are not. He had not married, even though he was almost fifty. Shubhojit and Debnath had been were his pals from his school days. It was unusual for people to continue keeping in touch with each other for on many years and to remain good friends for decades was rare. Shubhojit had persuaded him to go on a vacation and Debnath arranged everything regarding the trip, starting from the passport. So, here he was, peering out of the window at the sleeping town of Pattaya.

Jimmy was right, by Jove! He thought. This town was indeed asleep even though it was well into the morning. Then what he had heard was true! This town stayed awake the whole night, and slept throughout the day. All shops were closed. There were very few people on the street. The most striking thing that Shivam noticed was that he could see no school children on the street running towards their schools, satchels on their backs.

The tour operators held them on a tight leash. Time was the essence and punctuality, the virtue of kings. Right after breakfast they had been shooed into their tourist bus and whisked away from a drowsy Bangkok into the sunny but sleeping Pattaya. But the problem was that they were not even allowed to check-in, as presumably, the check-in time in the hotels was twelve noon. So they had been ferried off to visit the Coral Islands.

That trip had stirred his imagination no end. As he had no head for heights, he had wished away from the para-sailing stuff over the seas, but the underwater walk was a different kettle of fish altogether. He had gone into it with a quaking heart. Like many of the citizens of Kolkata, he had never learnt to swim and had stayed away from water all his life. He had no idea that the real thing could be so wonderful. It had felt as if he had been transported into a different world, where all was greenish blue. The bright sun above had lit up the aquatic world below with an aquamarine iridescence. The ochre and orange corals, the aquatic plants, the shoals of tiny fish, all added to the incredible sense of joy. It was here that he had first noticed Mandira. She was gripping his right hand in the human chain they had formed underwater, with all her might, as if her life depended on it. He had not minded, though. The touch and the grip were not at all unpleasant. But he felt a bit awkward or ridiculous, with the huge pot of running oxygen on his head and he standing out there with a naked torso, in the briefest of brief shorts. This was not the best place or outfit to meet a pretty girl, although the environs were idyllic. Tiny silvery fish nibbled through the entire slice of bread that their underwater guide had provided them with, and were nibbling at his fingers when he had come back to his senses. The guide tugged at his arms to indicate that they were going back up and up they went one by one. Once aboard the boat, and dried up and dressed, he gave her a sheepish grin. She too smiled back. Her teeth were even and pearly white. Her eyes lit up when she smiled. His world lit up too.

"It was wonderful down there, no? Like a different world!" Her voice was musical and enunciations clear.

"Yes, I loved it. It was the experience of a lifetime."

"Indeed it was."

They had to go in a single file to step back into the smaller boat that had been ferrying them all over the sea and this precluded the possibility of continuing their conversation, much though he would have liked to. This crossing over into the boat bobbing on the waves, was something that he hated. He crossed over very gingerly, but safely. She was standing there, all smiles.

"You were so nervous." she said laughingly.

"I don't know how to swim." he replied with a smile.

"Ah, I thought as much."

"You?"

"I am an aquatic animal." Her infectious laughter sounded like the tinkling crystals of a chandelier.

"Oh, by the way, I am Mandira Roy, from Kolkata."

"Bengali!"

"Oh yes. One hundred percent, unadulterated."

"I am Shivam Banerjee," he said.

"From Kolkata?"

"Yes."

Mandira was an Assistant Professor of English in a reputed college in Kolkata. She had come for a vacation to Thailand and would be going next to Malaysia and then to Singapur. She was with her parents. An elderly couple nodded from the opposite seat. Shubhojit and Debnath nudged at each other and looked away with a smile. A sudden wind whipped a lot of spray on their faces.

It was well into lunch time, when they came back to the mainland. Their guide took them straight over to a restaurant that served Indian food and they had a wonderful buffet lunch, though Shivam would have preferred some good, authentic Thai dish. Once lunch was over, Shivam went outside to enjoy a quiet smoke. Mandira joined him.

"The food was good." She observed.

"Yes, it was."

Mandira was a good conversationist and Shivam was a very good listener. So it worked well. The topics ranged from tourism, through modern literature, to the economy of Pattaya.

"I don't see boudi?" Mandira asked. "Where have you kept her? Or have you come to enjoy Pattaya all on your own, you naughty man?" Shivam burst out laughing.

"There is no 'boudi' as you say. But I know where I keep her hidden," he said, patting the left side of his chest.

"Aha! You are one of the few intelligent people left, I see! But, jokes apart, you have a way with words, although you don't talk much. Not like me, anyway. Just look at me, talking away."

"No, no. I love to hear you talk."

"You do?" There were a few seconds of rare silence. "Are you a poet? I simply love poetry!" Shivam was surprised.

"Yes, I write poetry. But how did you guess?"

"From your speech and from the way you look at things."

"You are very perceptive."

The hotel was quite big and comfortable. Shubhojit and Debnath shared a room and Shivam had another, all to himself. Shivam knew that his friends were very much interested in tasting the nectar of Pattaya. But these things did not interest him much. He had always been by himself but never lonely. Of course, now he was not even alone.

Mandira waited for him in the lobby. As luck would have it, they were on the same floor of the hotel. They went out together for a stroll. As they came out of the hotel, a signboard in Hindi, in front of what appeared to be a tea-stall across the road, caught his attention. He asked Mandira to stop and went over to the stall. The lady was very courteous and spoke to him in Hindi. Yes, she had Indian tea, Indian Coffee and Indian cigarettes to sell. Shivam had a coffee and Mandira some tea. They were enjoying themselves immensely. They laughed together, even at the little things they saw. For the first time in his life, Shivam was laughing with someone. They exchanged tales of their past, their likes and dislikes, their problems, small and big. Sitting in deck chairs near the beach, she made Shivam recite a poem he had written that morning. He had typed it painstakingly in his cellphone in the bus. So he could recite the whole poem. Shivam generally forgot what he had written. But now the problem did not arise. After listening to the poem, she sat quietly for a long time looking out at the sea. Shivam had given her his cell number, to be used in an emergency. By the time they returned in the evening, they were holding hands.

Shivam's phone rang. The caller ID showed a local number. When he heard Debnath's voice, he remembered that his friends had procured a local SIM card each from their guide right after reaching Bangkok Airport. His friends were going for a show. Shivam had heard about such Thai or Russian shows and did not find the idea exciting. He told Debnath that he was not interested.

"What about some booze afterwards?" Debnath asked.

"I am game enough for that."

"Ok, meet us at the bar near the beach we saw this morning at around 8 at night. We'll be there. You remember the place?"

"Oh yes." Shivam said.

"Good," his friend said. "From there we go for a walk down Walking Street."

"Great. I am game."

Walking Street was a dazzling place with brightly lit up garish signs and bill boards all over. People, mostly tourists, thronged it in thousands. Scantily clad but heavily made-up girls and boys dressed and made up like girls lined both sides of the street with blaring music in the background. Sex was on sale, but there was no haggling, soliciting or other such disturbances that one comes to expect in such places. The place throbbed with life and excitement. Shubhojit and Debnath ogled about them in wonder, looking rather like a youngster standing in front of a shop window, before Christmas. Both led a sedate and predictable life of upper middle-class gentlemen. Now they were on a true vacation.

A breeze from the sea brought with it a whiff of something frying. This smell was familiar and, to Shivam, was not altogether unpleasant. This same smell had assailed their nostrils as they were coming out of the bar. A big cart was parked next to the kerb, where things were being fried and sold. A sizable crowd had gathered around, mostly youngsters, tasting the morsels. Shivam had sidled over to find out what was cooking. Piles of scorpions, frogs and some indeterminate bugs lay in the dull copper sheen, waiting to be tasted with some sauce or whatever. The scorpions were looking sinister, complete with their hooked tails, even in death. The tiny frogs looked gruesome, frozen as if in the act of leaping. In spite of an initial queasiness, Shivam was game enough to try some and would have done so, had Shubhojit not puked in a roadside gutter.

This smell, mingling with the strong smell of perfumes, sweat, barbeque and alcohol, was heady, to say the least. Starry eyed Shubhojit and Debnath appeared smitten, but Shivam suddenly felt dead tired. He left his friends to continue their walking down Walking Street, and went outside the area to hail a cab. Then it started to rain. Not just rain, it literally poured.

The rain had abated a bit when Shivam reached his hotel. Even then he was drenched to his skin by the time he had paid the fare and rushed off to the shelter of the hotel foyer. Mandira flashed him a smile as she followed her parents into the ground floor restaurant.

Shivam could not stay put in his hotel room for long. He dried himself and changed into a red T-shirt, faded jeans and sneakers and came out of his room, locking his door behind him. Mandira came out of the elevator with her parents. Shivam nodded towards the elderly couple. Mandira's mother eyed him with suspicion. Mandira flashed another smile and stepped away. Shivam entered the elevator.

It had stopped raining. The broad leaved potted plants, lining the driveway, were still dripping. The driveway was thoroughly wet and the glistening surface reflected the light of the sodium vapour lamps gave the idea of a fairy land. Though not really hungry, Shivam was feeling a bit peckish. He stepped into towards the wide world outside. The stall where they had tea and coffee that afternoon was closed. Three girls huddled in the little shade that the closed stall offered, whispering to each other in morose tones. They were scantily clad. They huddled together waiting for customers, who never came their way along the wet street. By now a familiar whiff of something frying, titillated Shivam's senses. A similar cart to the one he had seen on the beach was parked in the nearest street corner. But the edibles were different. True, some octopi were being fried, yet the bulk was sausages, rolls and such familiar goodies. Shivam ordered some sausages and lit a cigarette while he waited for them to be fried. A girl dressed all in black, came up and ordered something in her native tongue. Sensing Shivam's eyes upon her, she looked up. Shivam drew in his breath. He had never seen eyes like those. They were large, and black and deep, oh, so deep! All Shivam could see in those eyes was pain, deep seated pain. The girl smiled a sad smile at him and lowered her eyes. She had seen deep compassion in the eyes of this stranger. The girl's order was ready earlier and as she paid for it, there was a lonesome tinkle of a few coins in her purse. She took out the coins, counted them and put them back after paying the shopkeeper. Shivam took his sausages and moved over along the driveway of the hotel to enjoy them as he walked up and down. Soon they were finished and Shivam walked out again, wiping his hands on his hanky.

The girl in black was sitting alone on a stool on the pavement. No customer had come and the other girls had probably gone home frustrated. But she was sitting there still, looking around in eager expectation. Shivam went up to her. Her eyes lit up when she saw Shivam.

"I knew you'd come." she whispered.

"Do you know English?" Shivam asked.

"Yes, a little bit." she answered.

"The others are gone. Why didn't you leave?"

The girl shrugged a pitiful little shrug.

"I couldn't. I had to stay."

"But why?" Shivam was persistant.

"I have no money."

"For food tomorrow?" The girl nodded in silence.

"Who else is there at home?" Shivam asked.

"My daughter...and mom."

Shivam sighed. She was sitting here for a customer, not merely to pay off a pimp, but to earn something so that she could feed her young one.

"This rain...see..." She gestured with her left hand towards the wet asphalt.

"I understand." said Shivam. "Can I help you with some money?"

The girl shook her head.

"You are very good. But I can't take your money just like that. For service, yes I can take. But not just like that. I am not a beggar, you see. I am so sorry. You are very good."

Shivam was astounded at her self-respect and stood there, moved, as she wiped her moist eyes irritably on the sleeve of her shirt.

"You'll come with me? Stay the night? I'll give you your fees and more. Come."

Shivam suddenly came awake at night. His mobile showed him that it was 2.15 a.m. Apart from the steady hum of the air conditioner, the room was quiet, except for a steady deep breathing coming from the far end of the wide bed. Shivam closed his eyes and drifted back to sleep.

The alarm woke him up at 6.30 a.m. Outside it was broad daylight. There was no one else in the room. The other side of the bed was neatly arranged. He stood up and padded over to the washroom to freshen up.

After coming back and ordering a cup of strong coffee over the intercom, he sat at the writing desk. An idea was brewing in his brain. He had to pen it down before it got lost in the mundane daily schedules. This morning, they would be leaving after breakfast to return to Bangkok. As he sat there, the hotel stationery caught his attention. A long note had been scribbled down on the writing pad with pencil. He picked it up and read.

"Dear stranger, I don't know your name. But you had come last night like an angel. You see, for three nights running it had rained hard. The streets were all wet. I had no customers. What little money I had was almost spent. If you had not come I would not have been able to buy baby food for my child. You were my angel. Like other men you had not abused me or used my body badly. I hate all men. But not now. You are not my angel. You are my God. I could not sleep well. It is 3.45 am now. As soon as sun rises I shall leave. We shall never meet again." The note ended suddenly as if the author had become overwhelmed by some strange emotions. Shivam sat holding the note in his hand. He then tore it off, folded it and shoved it into his wallet he habitually kept under his pillow. All bank notes and credit cards were intact. The woman had left, leaving behind a strange, hollow memory. He did not even know her name.

The message tone in his mobile beeped. Some sms had been sent from an unknown Indian number. The coffee came in at that same moment. He sat down with his cup and opened his inbox. The message was terse and brief.

"Had no idea that u were this type of a person. Saw a girl leaving ur room at 5.30 a.m. Am upset. Very much. Dont contact me again. Mandira."

Shivam smiled a sad smile. He sat still reading the message over and over again. Then he saved the number and typed the name 'Mandira'. After that he composed a brief message and sent it to this number.

Mandira was sitting still beside her open window. A gentle breeze was blowing in from the sea, somewhat soothing her hot, flushed cheeks. It was then her message tone beeped. She opened the message. The sender's name read "Shivam". In the text, only a single phrase had been typed 'When You Are Old...' Mandira sat still staring at the screen of her mobile. It was the title of the poem Shivam had recited for her. Her memory was painfully sharp. The last few lines of the poem, as recited by the poet, reverberated in her mind.

Even now if you feel all joy's on the wane
In fountains of happiness, there's somewhere some pain,
Do keep it in mind that I'm there with a balm
To ward off all hurt, make turmoil calm.
Don't think I'm a cloud to cut off sunshine.
I've a little shade to offer, for in pain you're mine.
Even when you grow old, an' fear end's near,
Even then at some crossroads you'd find me, my dear.

Two tear drops raced down her cheeks, rolling down unheeded, like twin pearls.

Her telephone rang suddenly, bringing her back to the present. She wiped her eyes and lifted the receiver. It was her father ringing from the next room.

"Are you ready, child?" He asked.

"Yes, father," she whispered. "Almost."

Shivam locked his door behind him and walked down the corridor towards the elevator with his trolley bag. It was time to check out.

✦ ✦ ✦

17

Atithi Devodaya

"Oil of Nine Gems!" Surabhi read on the label of the bottle. She poured a large quantity of the fabled 'head-cooling', perfumed, mentholated oil into her palm and dabbed it on her head. "Nine gems indeed! How very comforting! As if seven isn't enough!" thought she, as she vigorously massaged the oil into her scalp. They were seven. Seven of them barging into the sanctity of her household – a veritable tsunami in her peaceful lagoon!

Surabhi was a school teacher in a quaint little town in north Bengal. She taught History in an English medium school. Her husband, Utpal, was the manager of a nationalized bank. Their two daughters were both school going kids, one was in class IX, the other in class V. It was a happy family.

The summer vacations had started a week back. Surabhi had wanted to go somewhere during the holidays, but no programme could be made because Utpal could not get away from his bank. So they were reconciled to spending the holidays at home. Maybe towards the end of their vacation he would be able to snatch a few days' leave. Then they would go to the idyllic Dooars. Three or four days spent in a forest bungalow would be a refreshing experience.

Tanushree had called the day before their vacations started. They were coming to visit them. Tanushree was a distant cousin of Utpal. Once they had been quite close, but had lost touch over the last decade or so. Tanushree and her family stayed in Benaras. Her in-laws had their ancestral home in the holy city. Her father in law, Mahesh, had all but retired and it was her husband, Atul, who looked after their family business now. They were still a joint family of seven, Atul, Tanushree and their two kids, Atul's newly married younger brother and his wife and Mahesh, the head of the family. Atul's mother, a long standing diabetic, had passed away about five years back

They were coming by the late night train which arrived at around three in the morning. Surabhi had worked till late into the night making the beds and getting their house ready to receive the guests. At first she was at her wits end as to where to put all of them up. Their's was a modern flat that cut everything off to the barest minimum and space was the thing that had been the first casualty. But she was a good organizer and all was made ready. After all the guests would not stay for long, though she was not very sure about the exact length of their stay. In any case, she should not grumble, for it is said that guests are like gods.

The doorbell rang in unison with the old fashioned clock in the dining room chiming four in the morning. Utpal had asked the guests to take rickshaws from the station as his own car was still at the workshop for maintenance. His car was too small anyway, to carry all of them down, together. Now they were here.

Bleary eyed smiles welcomed the guests, as they entered the house. Surabhi escorted them to the drawing room, which suddenly appeared to have become very small. All of them were chattering together as they had tea and biscuits. This was a grand reunion after a long, long time. Surabhi was seeing Sujata, Anil's wife, for the first time and she expertly went through the motion of taking her chin is her hand exclaiming, "Oh Ma! What a lovely bride!" Atul and Anil began clamouring for some more tea and as Surabhi was starting to get up to make some more tea (the first round was exhausted soon enough), disaster struck!

Tanushree suddenly remembered that a vital social obligation remained unfulfilled. She sternly ordered her two children, a son and a daughter, of about the same age as Surabhi's own children, to touch the feet of pishey and pishima. The son, Paltu, a chubby kid, bred exclusively (possibly) on chocolates, ambled across to fulfil his obligations, much to the chagrin of Utpal and Surabhi. He had little idea about the trajectory of his ample backside and as he bent over to do the needful, he knocked against the table housing a dainty porcelain flower vase. The table, with its long and spindly legs could not bear the onslaught and all but toppled over. The vase tottered, almost recovered, over-corrected itself, then rolled over and came down crashing. A shriek was heard, emanating from Tanushree. "It's nothing!" protested Surabhi, lying in her teeth, for the vase was her favourite. But, guests can do no wrong!

The fragments were cleared by Surabhi in a trice, more tea was brought and equanimity was soon restored. All of them now began to speak at once.

"Do you remember..."

"Last year there was..."

"You hadn't been to the wedding of..."

"By God, the Government should be..."

Surabhi's head began to throb. The new bride, Sujata, a very intelligent and perceptive girl, who had been silent all through this, went up to her and said.

"Didi, where is the washroom please?"

Surabhi jumped up and escorted her to her destination.

"Didi, all this must be very disturbing for you, na? I mean so many of us turning up at the same time; it must be very tiring for you."

"Na re Chhutki, you don't mind if I call you Chhutki, do you?"

"Oh no, not all! You know Didi, you remind me of my own didi."

"Do I?" Surabhi was instantly disarmed and won over.

"Yes you do." Sujata replied with a smile. Surabhi smiled too and pinched the cheeks of the younger girl.

Anil yawned after his second cup of tea. His wife had come back from the washroom.

"Boudi," said he. "Haven't slept a wink in train. Can I lie down a bit please?"

This was the cue Surabhi was waiting for. She promptly shooed all the guests into their respective beds and went back to her own bedroom to stretch her tiring back muscles. Utpal had gone to the toilet.

Breakfast was a disaster. Surabhi had laid out toast, butter, jam, omelettes and fruit juice for all. But Paltu, the roly-poly son of Tanushree, began wailing. Apparently he did not like toast. He wanted parathas. His sister kept on asking for some hot chocolate. Atul would have preferred something light, like a few chapattis and vegetables. Tanushree showed no preference and said that she could take in whatever was served to her, but would have liked some aloo paratha with achar best. Mahesh was not very fussy but wanted unsweetened milk and cornflakes. One had to be a bit particular about one's diet, he declared. After all he was no longer young! Anil's jaw muscles worked as he spread a liberal dose of butter over the toasts that Sujata had silently pushed towards him. Then as the flustered Sujata began to run towards the kitchen, he gave at Paltu a cold, stony look.

"Paltu, either you take what is served or go hungry this morning. As it is pishimoni is overworked. Don't add to her burdens. The same holds good for all of you. You people are worse than little children!"

"No, no Anil, it is nothing!" Surabhi was feeling embarrassed at Anil's outburst. "The fault is mine. I should have asked you what you would like for breakfast."

"You better stay out of this, Boudi." Anil replied tersely.

"Arre na re baba," Atul said. "No fault of yours at all. Here, Tanu, pass the butter, will you?"

By the evening Surabhi was totally drained. Lunch had been a great success, only because like an expert *maitre d'*, Surabhi had taken the orders beforehand. Paltu and his sister did not like fish but preferred chicken or mutton. Tanushree liked fish curry and rice, as did Atul, provided it was not too spicy. Mahesh liked vegetable soup and asked for some curd as well. Anil was ready for everything provided Surabhi prepared it herself. Sujata had no preference, but laid down one condition, that she be allowed to help Surabhi in the kitchen. So it was dal, *bhat, machher jhol* – fish curry, *mangsho*, some vegetable soup, curd and sweets for lunch and all were happy, including Surabhi's daughters, Malini and Panchali, who liked nothing better than *mangsho bhat* – mutton rice.

Three days later the guests went off for local sightseeing. Utpal had arranged an air conditioned vehicle for them. They left early that morning and all was quiet at home once again. Surabhi spent almost the whole day relaxing in bed.

"How long will they be staying?" She asked Utpal.

"No idea." Utpal had his laptop open and was working on God-knows-what. It was a Sunday and his bank was closed.

"Still, you could ask them, couldn't you? You see the state I am in!"

"Ok, I'll ask them this evening."

But in the evening it seemed as if a Tsunami had broken over the household. The guests returned, flushed, grimy and excited. All were talking at once about the exciting things they had encountered during their day. Anil took out his digicam and connected it to Utpal's laptop so that all could see the snaps he had taken. Laughter followed like a deluge at the different poses. Amidst all this, Panchali, Surabhi's younger daughter came in quietly to stand beside her mother, trying to draw her attention.

"What is it, dear?" Surabhi asked.

"Mummy, Paltu has broken my video game."

"Shhhh dear. Don't tell anyone. I'll get you a new one, ok?"

Panchali went away, satisfied. She knew that she could depend on her mother totally.

The next morning, at breakfast, Utpal picked up enough courage to broach the rather unwelcome subject of the guests' departure. But true to form, his approach to the subject was rather tenuous.

"Ahem!" He cleared his throat. "These days it is really difficult to get railway reservations."

"You are right, Utpal," said Atul enthusiastically. He turned to Tanushree and said,"You remember Tanu, this time we had reserved our tickets two months beforehand."

"And the year before, when we were planning a Hardwar trip, we couldn't get a ticket one and a half months before date of journey." added Anil.

"Yes," Tanushree said. "Ultimately we had to cancel our trip."

"Yes, that's why I was thinking..." Utpal tried again.

"Enough of thinking!" Mahesh had sat up by this time. "This thinking stuff has brought our country to where it is now. In the British times it was different. People then acted. We got our Independence through action, not thought!"

"No, actually I was saying that regarding the Railway..."

"Ah, Utpal, don't talk about the Railways. See they don't allow a price hike in tickets, all for the wrong reasons, but service is grossly compromised. So who suffers? The people, who else?" Atul had got excited. "And when someone tries to raise the fare, he loses his job! These politicians are only concerned about voters."

"Every service has gone to the dogs." Anil said. "Why blame the railways alone? Look at the airlines! How many airports are up to mark in our country?"

Utpal glanced at Surabhi, shrugged resignedly and mumbling something about getting late for office, left. The storm continued at the breakfast table, over fresh cups of tea.

Surabhi's lips smiled at everyone, but her eyes did not. They were tied up with her brain, which at that precise moment was calculating who did not like what in terms of food and what was to be prepared for lunch and dinner.

It is said that misfortune never comes alone. Therefore it is always very wise to keep the weather eye open at the advent of the first stroke of misfortune. It is like a thunderstorm in May. The cloud is first seen in the western sky, not more than the size of a fist. Soon it races across to cover the sky. Then a gust of cold wind blows after which the storm breaks out along with flashes of lightning, peals of thunder and torrential rain, destroying all that comes in its path. Mala'r ma, the domestic help, who used to come in twice daily to clean the house and wash the clothes and utensils, was sniffing and snivelling for a few days. Surabhi had not noticed it. Then one morning, suddenly she was absent. Her daughter, Mala, came to report that she was unwell and could not come. The roof seemed to come down on Surabhi's head. Now, after breakfast was prepared, as elaborately as usual, Surabhi had to run the washing machine, running to the kitchen at intervals to stir what was being cooked. True, Sujata helped as much as she could, but it was evident that she was not at all used to these household chores and was more often a hindrance than real help. But it was her gesture that Surabhi liked, so she allowed her to do what she could. Tanushree, as usual, chewed betel leaf or enjoyed unscheduled siestas, having declared beforehand that she had come to enjoy some well earned rest. Mahesh and Atul read newspapers and discussed the future of the world in general and India in particular, while Anil moved about the whole house and the neighbourhood with his assortments of cameras, shooting sometimes in still, sometimes in the video modes. Utpal disappeared every morning, earlier than usual, for his office. The children played together with occasional wails at the inadvertent breakage of playthings or pieces of furniture while Surabhi toiled and at intervals, massaged the 'Oil of Nine Gems' into her scalp to cool her head. Mala's mother, the domestic help, returned for duty after a layoff of about four days, and things showed a marginal improvement.

Surabhi could not contain herself any longer. At breakfast the next day, she suggested in a sweet voice.

"You folks must be bored stiff sitting in the house. You have come so far north. Why don't you make a trip to Darjeeling? It is quite close and Utpal could arrange for your hotels and things easily. He has a few very good friends there, you know."

The guests looked at each other. Anil was the first one to rise up to the bait, of course, prompted by a gesture from Sujata. Sujata had very expressive eyes.

"A wonderful idea! Darjeeling is a grand place for photography. Every season there is wonderful!"

"I'd love it!" Sujata said, although she generally preferred to remain silent. "I have never been to Darjeeling."

"Ah well..." said Atul.

"Hmmm...." said Mahesh.

So it was all settled. Utpal practically ran to grab his cell phone, being put on charge in the bedroom and called the branch manager in the Darjeeling branch of his bank. Everything was settled in a trice, including booking the bank's Holiday Home for a week. The guests were to depart early next morning.

Peace reigned once again. Surabhi got a well earned rest and, to the chagrin of her daughters, focussed once again on their homework. Utpal had applied for leave near about the next weekend and he was sure that it would be sanctioned. They now began to plan for their Dooars trip in earnest.

Three days of uninterrupted peace was perhaps more than enough. Utpal had departed for his office to make all arrangements regarding his leave. He would also be booking the forest bungalow and organize a vehicle. Surabhi had taken an early bath and was spreading out her towel to dry on a line strung in their wide veranda overlooking the main road, when three rickshaws came up the street, coming to a stop in front of their building. From the rickshaws emerged their seven guests one after another. None was missing.

"You see bouma," Mahesh had taken upon himself to be the spokesperson of his group. "They have declared an indefinite strike in the hills starting day after tomorrow. So we thought that we shouldn't take a chance and took the first bus out." He set down the empty tea-cup with elaborate care. What could Surabhi say? Could she ever say anything?

✦ ✦ ✦

18

Hemlata

Hemlata was happy. In general she was one of a joyous disposition, but now her happiness knew no bounds. This morning she had had her urine tested. The report had made her one of the happiest persons in the world. She had resolved to visit the doctor before he left for his clinic. This was going to be a social call. So she thought she should take some sweets with her.

For years together she had been selling fish in the market of this quaint little hill town. She loved it here. Her home, in a basti, quite far away never deterred of dawn her from opening her shop on time. Every morning she left for work before the first light of dawn and walked over to the market. A stray dog that had made her front steps his home, wagged his tail vigorously when she emerged, and walked with her part of the way. These creatures were very much territorial. He never ventured far along the main road, but stood on guard, at a distance of some two hundred yards or so along the road, panting with a pink tongue hanging out and big bushy tail wagging. This was the point where he waited for her every night when she returned. He was a stray, but extremely well behaved and clean. Hemlata loved him as her own, but could not take him in because her husband could not tolerate animals of any kind. So, there he stayed, right outside her threshold, watching over her, day and night. Affectionately she called her King. She had kind of adopted him ever since he was a small puppy. She had discovered him on a cold winter night, whimpering under a pile of wood stocked near the railway station. He was alone, abandoned and she was not abandoned but lonely. So they instantly took to each other. That was about three years ago. Now he had grown rather big and black, a typical representative of the sturdy kind that are found only in these hills.

Everyone called her 'Didi'. It was a great thing that didi meant the same in her native Nepalese as well as the Bengali language. It meant elder sister. She loved being called Didi. About half her customers were Bengali. But this was to be expected. Bengalis are reputed to be fish eaters the world over and she sold fish. It also helped that she could speak passable Bengali as well, for though most of her regular customers were fluent in Nepalese, they loved being addressed in their mother tongue. She did not thank her stars for being able to talk in it. She thanked the monks of the Ramakrishna Mission instead.

Her father had been as poor as a church mouse. He worked as a porter near the railway station. He worked like a man possessed from dawn to dusk, seldom if ever, stopping even for lunch. All day he ferried goods on his back in his *dhukpa,* strapped to his forehead by means of ropes or leather thongs, or carried them directly strapped against his forehead, if they were too large. He carried vegetables and fish unloaded by the goods trains to the market, or luggage for the railway passengers, or fuel like coal and firewood, or even furniture, when people bought them or were moving house. At intervals he used to sit on the parapet beside the railway tracks, where the lines curved like a scimitar before entering the station, chatting wearily with his fellow porters, puffing cheap, unfiltered cigarettes one after another. Towards the evening he used to leave for home. On his way back he used to spend about a fourth of what he had earned during the day on local cheap whiskey, called Roxy, and plodded home, usually half drunk. He never behaved badly with his wife and children even when he was dead drunk. He worked like a man possessed because he wanted to provide basic education to his children. He had two, a beautiful daughter called Hemlata, and a son. He was illiterate himself, as was his wife and so they knew the true value of education.

Both Hemlata and her brother used to attend the free primary school run by the monks of the Ramakrishna Mission. From her childhood, Hemlata had been a bright student. This had drawn the attention of her teachers, all of whom were Bengali monks and they took turns to give her special coaching in that subject. She could recite several poems written by Rabindranath Tagore, Satyendranath Dutta and even Kazi Nazrul Islam.

One day, her father died. She was a student of Class VIII at that time and her brother was in Class VI. Over the last few days he had been running a fever, not a very high one, but weakening nevertheless. But he went out and worked even though he was ill. Then he began coughing blood. The doctor in the hospital said that he had contracted tuberculosis and his condition was serious. He arranged for his admission to the sanatorium, but he refused, carrying on with his work as usual. Then, one day he began to cough blood in large quantities. Within two days he was gone. Her mother was a strong woman. She had the last rites performed, wiped her eyes and took to caring for her children. She took up the job of a maid in a local hotel. To supplement her meagre income, which could barely sustain the family, she had to go out at nights sometimes to entertain guests.

Within a couple of years she gave her daughter away in marriage. Her son, drifted away even before finishing school and the last she had heard of him was that he was working as a cab driver in a town the foothills.

For the first four years of her married life, Hemlata walked on clouds. Her husband owned a tiny stall in the local fish market and business was good, so they were more or less well off, at least compared to many other families in her basti. Often she went with him to help in his business and she loved it. Her husband loved her, so did her in-laws. But this love appeared to be on the wane later on, when she had failed to conceive even in the fifth year of their marriage. After that they went to a doctor. The doctor, an elderly general practitioner, listened to their tale of woes, examined her and wrote out some medicines, but months went by without any result. Their lives became barren in more senses than one.

Then they went to the big town in the foothills. There the gynaecologist conducted a whole lot of examinations and investigations, before declaring that she was perfectly normal, while he would never father a child unless he took the specified treatment. Hemlata urged her husband to take the courses of treatment regularly, but he simply gave up. The situation changed from bad to worse as he became grumpy and later, took to booze and other women. Her nagging in-laws too, fell silent and there was no one who could share her sorrow. Her mother had remarried and moved to another town far away in the hills. She was alone. Her husband began neglecting his business and financially too the family started going downhill. It was at this juncture when she met her one-time teacher near the market. She told him everything. He advised her to come to the Mission once in a while and start of managing their shop in the market. The sessions at the Mission provided great solace to her wounded soul and the fish market provided her with comfort. Laughter returned to her lonely life and soon enough she became Didi to all.

"Didi, you look so happy today, almost radiant!" The girl selling dried fish near her shop accosted her. "What's the secret? Tell me."

Hemlata smiled and efficiently changed the topic. After nearly twenty years of marriage, if she said that she was happy because she had sex with her husband last night, who would believe her? She hummed a Rabindra sangeet as she vended fish all day, much to the pleasant surprise of her clientele.

"Didi, o Didi!" Doctor didi was leaning over from her veranda of the house right in front of her shop was calling her.

"Yes Didi?" she replied.

"Have you got some fresh fish for me?"

"Oh yes." Hemlata picked up a particularly good specimen and held it aloft for her to examine. "Take this one Didi."

"Ok, cut it up and keep it ready. I'm coming down."

The doctor couple, with their little daughter had come to live in this house for about three years now. They were very good people. Both of them worked in the nearby hospital and their daughter had been admitted recently to a good English medium school. Every morning the Doctor didi escorted their daughter to the jeep that carried her to school and on her way back she picked up her requirements from the market, exchanging pleasantries with the shopkeepers. Everybody liked her sunny disposition. Her husband, Snehashis, the doctor, was a bit more reserved, but very courteous and a true gentleman. Both of them spoke fluent Nepalese and none of the locals ever thought that they were outsiders.

A month and a half later, Hemlata called on Doctor didi. She could barely contain her happiness.

"Didi," Hemlata asked. "When can I see dada in his chamber?"

"He is at his clinic right now. Do you have a patient?" Doctor didi asked.

"Yes," Hemlata was almost blushing. "I am the patient."

Doctor didi was elated. She grabbed Hemlata's shoulder and looked into her face closely. Then she smiled and hugged her hard, despite the smell of fish that came from her body and clothes.

"Oh Didi, I am so happy for you." She knew of Hemlata's woes. "Did you get your urine tested?"

"Not yet. I'll consult dada first and do as he suggests." Doctor dada was a gynaecologist. When Hemlata went away to see the doctor, she seemed to be dancing rather than walking.

As was expected, Snehashis had advised her to get her urine tested. The results made her the happiest person in the world. The word "Positive" was typed out in bold letters. She ran straight to the doctor's home, having picked up a box of sweets on her way, but he had already left for his clinic. Doctor didi, too was not at home. So she dumped the box of sweets on the dining table, issued some instructions for the amazed domestic help and ran off. She skipped across the railway tracks, up the busy sloping road that led to the doctor's chamber, close to the hospital and burst into his clinic.

"Dada," she cried, regardless of the flabbergasted patient who was sitting on the chair across the doctor.

"Didi!" The doctor looked up from whatever he was writing. "Is all ok?"

"Oh yes, dada. Look, the result has come 'Positive'!"

"Oh Didi," the doctor jumped off from his chair. He moved over to where Hemlata stood in ecstasy, snatched the report from her hand and read it. "Now, Didi," he said in a falsely severe tone. "You go straight home and lie down. You need rest. Take the vitamins that I prescribed earlier and plenty of fluids too. But rest, you need a lot of rest."

The telephone rang just as Snehashis was finishing his lunch. He picked up the receiver. He listened in silence to whatever the person was saying from the other end. The receiver slipped from his nerveless fingers to the carpeted floor. Payel, his wife came running.

"What's wrong?" she anxiously asked. "Who called?" She replaced the receiver into the cradle.

"Roy." Dr. Roy was the Pathologist.

"What did he say? Why are you so upset?" Payel asked.

"Hemlata's report is actually negative. He had wrongly given her someone else's report. He checked and cross checked thrice. Said that he was very sorry. Probably she is approaching an early menopause."

Hemlata was sitting still. Payel was sitting beside her on a bench in a children's park. She was holding Hemlata's cold, clammy hands in her own hands. Tears rolled down Hemlata's cheeks. Payel's eyes brimmed over. Hemlata sat silently for a long time. Payel too, did not speak a word.

"Didi," Hemlata asked, "Dada could have given me the news himself, couldn't he? He could have telephoned. I had given him my number. But he didn't. He sent you over to inform me. Why Didi? He could not face me, is that it? But why? He is not at fault. Yet he could not face me. Why Didi? Why are people so compassionate? Why?" She was crying openly now. Tears ran down her cheeks unchecked. It started raining. Neither Payel, nor Hemlata opened their umbrellas. The tears were washed away by the pelting raindrops.

✦ ✦ ✦

Glossary

Glossary of relations used in the stories:

Beta	Son
Boudi	Brother's wife
Bouma	Daughter-in-law
Chacha	Father's younger brother
Chachi	Father's younger brother's wife
Dada / da	Brother
Daju	Elder brother
Maa	Mother
Pishey	Father's sister's husband
Pishima	Father's sister
Pishimoni	Father's sister lovingly